NEAR and DEER

SYLVIA LIU

SCHOLASTIC INC.

ISBN 978-1-339-01018-2

10 9 8 7 6 5 4 3 2 1   24 25 26 27 28

Printed in the U.S.A.   40

First printing 2024

Book design by Maeve Norton

To Susan and Alan,
with much love

CHAPTER ONE

Making a banana chocolate chip muffin is a perfectly choreographed dance. It has to be, because the breakfast part of the Rolling Hills Bed & Breakfast is all up to me this week. My parents are out of town touring other inns, checking out the competition, and only Nainai—my grandma—is around.

I review my list:

Gather equipment: Mixing bowls. Spatula. Sifter. Hand mixer. Muffin tins. *Check.*

Collect ingredients: Sugar. White and wheat flour. Vegetable oil. Chocolate chips. Bananas. Eggs. Milk. Salt. Baking soda. *Check.*

Turn on the oven and set to 400 degrees. *Check.*

If I time everything right, I'll be done mixing the muffin batter just as the oven is ready. This is what I love: Sienna Chen in charge. I'm in control of my space, ingredients, and timing, and there's nothing to distract me from—

WOOF!

A bundle of energy in the form of a sheepadoodle bounds into the kitchen. Just my luck that my dog interrupts me. But I can't get mad at his adorable, open-mouthed grin. "Jules!" I crouch down and give his head and shoulders a vigorous rub. "Good morning!" I snuggle my face into the shoulder of my best friend in the whole world.

Some people might think Jules is your average sheepadoodle—a cross between a shaggy Old English sheepdog and a standard poodle, but really, he's the cutest sheepadoodle to ever exist. He has fluffy and curly fur, with black and white patches all over his body. His face is also a patchwork, with black ears and eyes and a white snout. His paws are like little mops. When guests meet him for the first time, they think he's a living stuffed animal. So, naturally, they fall completely in love with him.

Jules licks my face and wags his tail so hard his entire back half makes a scrabbling dance across the tile floor. If he could talk, I'm pretty sure he'd be saying, *Sienna, come play! I want to go outside!*

Sure enough, Jules runs out of the room, and in moments comes back with his favorite toy, a squeaky manatee. He drops it at my feet and looks up with his doggy grin.

"I want to play, Jules," I say, "but I have to make these muffins. We'll play after I finish breakfast and serve the guests. To the corner."

Jules normally pays attention and will wag his tail and settle himself on the blanket, but instead, he stands at the door and paws at it insistently.

"Want to go outside?" I open the kitchen door and let him out. Jules careens down the slope to the trees at the bottom of the hill, past the chicken coop and the goat barn. That's odd—he usually sticks closer to the inn.

At the tree line, a flash of brown and white moves, then it's gone. Maybe it's a deer. One or two have been coming by almost every day this week.

I sigh and go back to mixing the muffin batter. I'll never get used to living in the middle of nowhere in Virginia farm-and-forest country. Six months ago, Mom and Dad threw away our perfectly normal life in the D.C. suburbs—friends, softball, and a neighborhood with a bike path—and took all their savings and bought this inn, chasing Mom's dream of living a simpler life. But, of course, it's not simpler! It's a whole lot of work. Did they think about that when they moved? Did they ask me what I thought? No, and no.

I'd been having a tough time with my friends in D.C.—they'd stopped inviting me over, saying I was too bossy—but before I could fix things with them, we'd moved. Now I have no friends *and* I'm feeding chickens, milking goats, and making up beds for guests. It's so different from what I was used to, but at least I have Jules—he's the best friend anyone could have. We love exploring the woods nearby. I can always depend on him, and his pure joy at having so much space to run around always cheers me up.

Nainai bustles into the kitchen. "Good morning, Sienna. Look at you, up so early." My grandma grabs a pineapple to slice. She expertly chops off the ends and sides with a large cleaver. Nainai's superpower is picking fruit at the exact peak of ripeness, so her cut fruit is always perfectly sweet and not overdone. I know I'm spoiled by her fruit-picking prowess. Anywhere else, watermelon slices are too mealy or cantaloupe is terribly hard and bland.

I look up from folding the chocolate chips into the batter. "Good morning, Nainai." Normally, we Chens have the breakfast routine down pat. On weekends, Nainai prepares fresh fruit with yogurt, I make a breakfast pastry, and Mom and Dad take turns with the hot breakfast, whether it's eggs or pancakes or waffles.

Today is Sunday—no school—but with Mom and Dad away, Nainai is taking care of the hot foods and I have the added tasks of feeding the chickens and goats, which Dad usually handles. My thoughts churn. New tasks mean mental juggling and more worries.

I can't mess anything up. Mom and Dad are on a quest to land the Star Innkeepers seal, to join the exclusive club of highly sought-after inns, so I have to do everything possible to help them, which means giving our guests the best experience. I place the muffins in the oven and set a timer.

As Nainai cuts the pineapple, I notice she's cutting them in a more triangular shape than normal. "Nainai, not like that. You need to cut them the way you always do."

Nainai looks up and smiles. "I change things up so I don't get bored."

"Why do we need to change things now, especially when Mom and Dad aren't home? It's not time to go wild." This is the worst time to break routine; new variables mean new ways things can go wrong. "Plus, we have more guests coming today." We already have two couples, and now two more people are coming to stay long-term, for a month—a scientist and her son. The thought of having to be pleasant to guests for longer than a day or two is honestly exhausting.

Nainai laughs. "I'm hardly going wild by cutting the pineapple into triangles."

"But it could be a choking hazard, and it's going to take you more time to cut them smaller, and you need to get started on the pancakes, and I have to get the drinks and juices going." I know it sounds silly to worry about details like this, but I can't help it. My stomach clenches at the thought of my growing to-do list. "And I need to gather the eggs, feed the goats and chickens, and cut fresh flowers."

"Sienna, take a breath," Nainai says. "We don't need to do everything at once. You work on the muffins. The animals can wait." My grandma stretches, then winces, holding her lower back.

"Are you okay?"

"I think so. I might've tweaked something. I'll go lie down." Nainai scoops the pineapple into a serving dish. "When the muffins are done, please set everything on the sideboard. The guests will be down soon. I know you can handle the breakfast and make it a star-worthy experience."

I gulp. It's great that Nainai trusts me so much, but it's an important responsibility. I have to get everything just right. I take out some plates to set the tables.

WOOF! WOOF!

Jules is back at the door, barking urgently.

"What now?" I set the plates down and get to my sheepadoodle.

Jules runs around in circles, barking sharply. It isn't his usual *let's play* bark, but rather an insistent yelp. He nudges me to usher me out the door.

"Okay, I'm coming." I brush the crumbs off my hands. The muffins will be ready in less than five minutes, but I'll just see what Jules wants and be back in no time.

I step out the side door that leads to the backyard and garden. Jules is already down past the goat pen and almost to the forest. He's agitated by something in the grassy area by the trees.

As he sees me, Jules runs back, his whole body shaking. The chickens in the fenced area outside the coop scatter, clucking in alarm.

"I'm coming, I'm coming."

My sheepadoodle turns and runs again to the woods past the goat pen, barking. There's no doubt. He wants me to follow him.

I glance back to the kitchen, then at Jules, and sigh. I still have so much to do, but I can tell Jules is serious. So I follow him down to the woods.

CHAPTER TWO

"Wait up, Jules!" I jog down the hill from the house, past the chicken coop and the goat pen. I reach the field that leads to the woods and tromp through the grasses that have grown past my knee.

Jules runs to me and tilts his head, his tongue lolling out. He turns and runs back to the end of the clearing near the woods. As he moves, parts of him peek out from the field, his tail wagging like a fluffy pirate flag in a sea of waving grass. I chuckle at the sight. "You're such a silly boy."

Jules barks again, this time more urgently. His snout and front disappear in the tall grass; his wiggling tail and backside are all that's showing. Jules runs around a spot and his bark turns into excited yips. He runs back and hustles me over. *Come on, human girl, hurry. Hurry. It's very important. You have to come.*

I wonder if he's dug up another treasure. One of Jules's favorite things since we've moved here is to dig up old coins and other things around the property.

"This had better be good, Jules." I follow him.

I approach slowly; I don't want to stumble into any snakes in the grass. Even though our neighbor Mr. Buchanan has explained most of the snakes around here, like black rat snakes, are harmless, I hate the idea of critters slithering below my feet.

As I reach the spot where Jules is bouncing around, I glimpse a bit of brown and white peeking through the grass.

Jules stands near it, smiling at me and as proud as could be, as if he's personally responsible for the sight in front of me.

It's a baby deer . . . a fawn!

The fawn is the cutest thing I've ever seen. It has big ears that stand at attention, large brown eyes, and a tiny body covered with white spots. It sits curled in a little ball in the grass and peers at Jules through long lashes and trusting eyes, not scared or fazed by him at all.

"Stay, Jules," I say softly. I try to calm my beating heart. I've never been so close to such a small fawn. My heart's about to burst, protectiveness and wonder surging through me. What a precious bundle!

The fawn notices me and stiffens, then trembles.

I crouch down slowly, holding my breath, and make myself as small and still as possible.

The fawn looks over to Jules, as if for reassurance, and Jules edges closer to it.

The animals stare at each other and bring their heads close. The fawn stands up, a little unsteady. It bleats a small *weah* and bumps its head into Jules.

My dog sniffs at the fawn, his mouth setting in a huge grin and his tail wagging like it's about to fall off.

That's when I see it: On the fawn's side, one of the spots is the shape of . . . a heart! My jaw drops open. How perfect is this? I think I've instantly fallen in love with this creature who has love stamped on its side.

"You found a fawn," I say. "It's the sweetest and most incredible thing I've ever seen."

Jules nuzzles at the fawn, who seems to like the attention.

"Come, Jules. Let's leave it alone." I look around. The momma deer might be hiding in the woods, scared off by the commotion Jules is causing. "Its mom might be near."

Jules doesn't pay attention to me. He nuzzles at the fawn. It seems comfortable with Jules and sits back down in the grass. Jules seems to know that it's a baby, because he walks around it gingerly, tail flapping back and forth.

He settles down next to the fawn and smiles again. The fawn looks up at me with what I swear is a similar expression. The two sit together as if posing for a family portrait, enjoying the sun.

I can't help but laugh. "You found a new friend," I say in a low, delighted voice. I could stay here forever, basking in this beautiful sight of instant besties. I take a mental snapshot, vowing to remember this magical moment.

I stiffen when I remember. The muffins! I've completely forgotten about them. "We have to go back!"

Jules tilts his head. I know he understands me, but he's being an ornery boy, saying, *I want to stay with my new friend. See how happy we are? Look! The fawn has put its head on my shoulder.* Sure enough, it has, and Jules tucks his head on the fawn's in return.

Not only are the muffins past done, but I haven't set the tables or gotten breakfast ready. The guests are probably already downstairs waiting. Nainai's probably not there to help them.

I edge closer to Jules, careful not to startle the fawn. I wonder why it doesn't get up and run away, since it did stand up briefly. I reach for Jules's collar, careful not to touch the fawn. "Jules, we really have to go," I say in a firmer tone.

This time Jules gets up, letting out a small whine.

The fawn looks at me with large, doleful eyes, and my heart cracks a bit. This little one's mom better come back soon.

I turn to the house, and Jules follows. As we leave the grassy area, Jules turns and lets out a growl.

I catch a glimpse of something in the woods. A movement of brownish red that flashes, then disappears. It seems like an animal, bigger than a fox. Sometimes a coyote hangs around trying to get at our chickens, and even a bear has shown up at night, but Jules usually keeps them away. Jules darts toward the trees, barking at whatever's lurking in the woods.

"Jules, come back!"

Jules comes reluctantly. I really have to get back

to the muffins. They might even be burning now. But—the poor fawn. Its mother doesn't seem to be around, and it'll be helpless against a predator.

I look to where the fawn sits hidden in the tall grass. "We'll come back later to check on you."

I swallow my worry and run back up to the inn.

I'm almost at the inn, by the chicken coop, when our neighbor Mr. Buchanan waves from his side of the fence. He's driving an ATV in his cornfield.

I wave back, and Jules lopes over to say hello.

"Let's not bother him, Jules." I glance at the inn. We don't have time to chitchat, but it'd be rude to ignore him. I go over, hoping to get away after a quick hello.

Mr. Buchanan is a wiry, older guy, wearing his usual faded checkered shirt and floppy hat. He gets off his ATV and scowls as he inspects a corn plant. He isn't the friendliest of neighbors, but I'm always polite to him. "Hello, Mr. Buchanan. Is everything okay?"

My neighbor shakes his head. "It's my vegetable garden. The darn deer are everywhere, and ruining them, even this early in the season."

He sounds just like Dad, who's always complaining

about the deer getting into our flowers. "Don't your fences stop them?"

"No, they're too wily," Mr. Buchanan says. "I'm gonna have to do something about those deer." His eyes narrow as he looks to the woods. "In fact, it's already done."

Something? He isn't a hunter, so he wouldn't shoot a deer, but the hard edge in his voice makes it sound like he has something terrible planned. The fawn! A chill goes down my back. What if something has happened to the little deer's mother and that's why she isn't around? I love seeing the deer pass through the woods and graze on the wild grasses at the edges of our land. They don't get into our family's garden thanks to Jules. He probably thinks they're there to play with him, but his barking and running always scares them off.

I'm about to ask Mr. Buchanan what he means by "doing something," but he's returned to his vehicle and driven off.

"Um, okay. Bye," I say to his back. I don't have time to puzzle out what he means. "Come on, Jules, we've gotta go." I have muffins to rescue.

CHAPTER THREE

I scramble into the house, Jules following at my heels. The kitchen door slams behind us.

I groan. The smell of burnt muffins oozes through the kitchen. Nainai's nowhere in sight.

What an epic disaster.

I shut off the oven and yank the oven door open. Smoke billows out. Jules runs around the kitchen, barking his head off.

The smoke alarm blares.

I grab some mitts and pull the muffins out, my eyes tearing up from the smoke. At least there doesn't seem to be flames. Jules keeps barking and pushes at my legs, trying to save me from danger. "It's okay, Jules"—I cough and try to catch my breath—"I'm alright."

The muffins are ruined, their tops blackened like tiny wastelands in a baked-goods apocalypse.

"What's going on? Is everything okay?" a voice calls out. One of the guests, a woman who's come with her daughter to visit colleges, stands at the doorway with a look halfway between concerned and horrified.

"Everything's fine!" I shout over the alarm. I brush my hair from my face, grab a broom, and jab the handle at the smoke alarm to turn it off. I grit my teeth and smile. "I'll be right out with breakfast."

The woman steps into the kitchen. "Are you by yourself? Let me help."

The alarm stops with a final jab of the broom. "I'm fine. My grandma's in the other room. She just stepped out for a moment." I give the woman my widest smile, though I'm sure I look like a wild child with my hair sticking out in all directions and smoke all around me.

The woman leaves with a dubious look.

I open the windows and shoo the smoke away. I slump against the counter, which is strewn with bowls, measuring cups, and muffin ingredients. I shake the burnt muffins into the trash, wash my hands, and grab the plates and place settings.

The woman and her daughter sit at one of the breakfast tables, and an older couple hovers by the dining room entrance. They've come from Tennessee to visit Virginia vineyards.

"Please, sit." I'm painfully aware the guests are staring as I set out the plates and silverware. I'm not any good at small talk, but now it's a hundred times worse trying to come up with something to say as the adults look on with pity. "I'll be back." I scurry to the kitchen.

Now I have to figure out what to serve them. We normally give guests a cute menu I've designed myself with breakfast choices like *Fabulous Farm Fresh Eggs*, *Waffles to Warm Your Heart*, and *Fruit and Yogurt Extravaganza*. But since I'm not allowed to short-order cook and Nainai is nowhere around, none of these options work. I toss the menus aside.

I rummage through the freezer and find a package of frozen bagels. I take some out and zap them in the microwave. No time to toast them. Scrounging through the fridge, I gather butter, leftover goat cheese Mom made from our goat milk, and a jar of store-bought jam.

My heart sinks at the sight of these sad spreads. If only I had time to pick some flowers for the tables, at least the breakfast would look nice. But everything's a cobbled-together mess, accented with the scent of burnt muffins.

Impatient rustling from the dining room prompts

me to hurry to them. After I serve the food, I slink back to the kitchen, but not before seeing the older woman's raised eyebrow at the untoasted bagel and overhearing her say, "This isn't what I had in mind when they advertised a gourmet breakfast."

Flashing lights spill into the room from the window outside.

A demanding knock on the door.

I peer out the window and clutch my stomach, a sudden ache stabbing my gut. A fire truck and an ambulance have pulled up to our inn.

The guests stand up, mill around, and exclaim. Jules runs to the door, barking.

I rush over and open the door to a serious-looking firefighter with a buzz cut and a weathered face.

"Are your parents here? We received an alarm from this property."

"Come in," I manage to squeak.

He steps over the threshold and cranes his neck toward the dining area. "I'm going to have to ask everyone to step out of the property. It's not safe to be on the premises when there's an alarm and evidence of a fire. What happened?"

I splutter. "There was a small fire in the oven, but it was mainly smoke and everything's okay now. Um, I'll go get my grandma."

The man nods curtly. "You do that, and my crew will take a look. Sandy will escort the guests out."

I feel like I'm going to be sick. The morning has gone from bad to worse. But I have to keep it together. I run to my grandmother's room.

Nainai sits on her bed, a groggy look on her face. "What's going on? I heard an alarm."

I gulp. "Everything's a mess." I quickly explain about the burnt muffins and the firefighters and emergency people at the inn.

"At least no one's hurt." Nainai pushes herself up, and groans. "Oof, my back. I'll go talk to them, but tell me, why weren't you watching the muffins?"

I want to explain why I messed up, but something stops me from telling Nainai about the fawn. Our encounter was such a magical moment. The fawn is a secret I want to keep for myself—like a gift the world has given me. Anyway, the fawn is probably gone by now, so there's no point bringing it up. "I'm so sorry. I was outside with Jules and got distracted."

"We'll talk about this later. I'll handle the firefighters."

Nainai manages to convince the firefighters that we're okay, though we have to listen to a lecture about fire safety. I apologize to the guests, who are clearly unhappy when they check out. Ugh. Now they're going to leave terrible reviews.

After they leave, my grandma goes back to lie down. "If your parents call, let's not mention the fire or my back," Nainai says. "We don't want them to worry. It's important they get the Star Innkeepers seal, so we shouldn't distract them. We'll tell them when they come back."

I'm relieved to hear her suggestion, since I'd rather explain in person too. "I'll clean up in the kitchen." I still have to feed the animals and check on the fawn.

"Please make sure the suite is ready for the new guests. They should be coming soon," Nainai says. Attached to the main inn is an addition with its own entrance—a suite with a large bedroom, a living room, and a kitchenette. It even has its own patio with a couple of rocking chairs. It'll be perfect for our long-term guests.

I give my grandma a hug. I have a lot to do, but

maybe going through my list of chores will help put the disastrous morning behind me.

After cleaning the kitchen, I go to gather eggs. On the way to the chicken coop, Jules bounds over and barks. He runs partway to the woods and looks back with an eager expression, tail wagging, as if to say, *Let's go back to the fawn. When else am I going to have such a cute friend to play with?*

"Not now, Jules." The field of wild grasses sways invitingly, but I have work to do. "Come back."

Jules seems torn, but he listens.

I throw cracked corn for the chickens and gather seven eggs from three nesting boxes. The knots in my stomach slowly ease as I greet my feathery friends.

Jules trots to the goat pen, saying hello to the goats that come to the fence.

Inside the barn, the familiar sweet smell of hay greets me. The goats, all girls, gather around, bleating and snuffling. It's like a goat-greeting party whenever I come by. "Hello, Mimi, Tabitha, Raven . . ." I usually love this part of the day, but as I scoop alfalfa hay and put it in their troughs, my mind churns over the kitchen disaster and the fawn.

While the goats are eating, I disinfect my hands and milk our two goats that have given birth this spring, Cocoa and Agatha. Soon I have almost two quarts of milk. Mom makes goat cheese and soaps and lotions out of the milk, which we use for recipes or sell to our guests. I bring the milk back to the house and transfer it into glass bottles.

Then I ready the suite for the new guests. I try to put the burnt muffins out of my mind as I fix fresh flowers for the suite and look up how to fold a towel into a deer shape. I've been making towel animals ever since our family went on a cruise a couple of years ago. This will surely impress guests and help my parents win the Star Innkeepers seal.

I frown. That little fawn better be okay. There might be a fox or coyote after it, and Mr. Buchanan might've done something to its mother. As soon as I'm done here, I'll go with Jules to check on the fawn.

CHAPTER FOUR

Thump. Thump. Thump.

Jules's tail wagging against the door to the suite alerts me to his presence. I prop the deer towel up on the bed and open the door. "What do you have there?"

Jules drops something on the porch—a dirt-encrusted, small metal object. Maybe a coin or token.

"You dug up another treasure?" Ever since we moved here, Jules has been bringing me his finds. There must've been a colonial settlement a long time ago in this area. At first, we worried Jules would swallow the treasures, but he's good about not doing that. I even got a metal detector for my birthday to help look for the artifacts.

I take the piece from Jules and lead him back to the inn and to my room. My parents and Nainai live in two bedrooms and a small common area off the kitchen, away from the guests, while I have a room in the lower level. It's technically a basement, but because the inn is on a slope, I have decent-sized windows, and it doesn't feel like I'm living in a hole.

"Good boy!" I scratch Jules under his chin, and he flops down at the foot of my bed. Between befriending the fawn and finding the coin, Jules must be having the best day of his life.

I rinse the dirt off the object. It turns out to be a penny from 1968—not the oldest coin he's found, but pretty good, so I put it in the shoebox of his finds. A couple of months ago, Jules found a really old piece of glass, and another time, he dug up part of an old ceramic plate. I look up those types of finds in my book *Discovering Virginia's Colonial Artifacts*, and put them in the display box on my dresser if they turn out to be valuable.

The doorbell rings, and Jules leaps up, barking, *There's a guest at the inn! There's a guest at the inn!* He runs around in circles, and I shut him in my room. Not everyone likes being greeted by a slobbery seventy-pound dog. Of course, those guests are cold, cold fish, because who wouldn't fall desperately in love with the bundle of black and white fluff that is Jules? But I've learned that not everyone—*gasp*—loves dogs.

I lope upstairs. The whiff of burnt muffins still

lingers, but there isn't anything to be done about it. I open the front door to find a woman with dark hair pulled back into a ponytail, wearing a light blue T-shirt, gray hiking pants, and boots—all of which look well-worn. Behind her, coming up the steps to the porch, is a boy who seems about my age, with similar thick brown hair, an eager smile. He's wearing athletic shorts and an *Avatar: The Last Airbender* T-shirt.

"Hi," I say. "Come in."

"Hello. You're a bit young to be an innkeeper." The woman's voice is friendly, and her eyes twinkle with amusement.

"My parents are the owners, but they're away, and my grandma is taking a nap."

The woman and the boy step into the foyer.

"Oh, this is so cool, look at the wallpaper and the paintings of rabbits, this reminds me of an old English hunting lodge, not that I know what an old English hunting lodge is," the boy says in a single-breath sentence.

"Come over to the sitting room, and I'll get you checked in." I lead them to the couches by a fireplace and built-in shelves, the central gathering place for guests. The shelves are white and overflowing with books and knickknacks, with cabinets below that hold games.

"I'm Susan Klein, and this is my son, Max." She looks around appreciatively. "This is so lovely. What a great base this'll be for the next month."

"She's *Dr.* Susan Klein," Max chimes in. "Mom's got a PhD in mycology—that's the study of mushrooms."

"You can call me Susan."

I've never heard of anyone who studies mushrooms. How much is there even to know about those things? But my job is to be welcoming and polite. "I'm Sienna Chen. I'll show you your rooms." I turn to the boy. "It's hares."

"Hares?"

"The paintings are of hares." Ever since Mom and Dad came back from their trip to England, they've added English country home vibes to the inn, with a cool wallpaper pattern of hares and vines, paintings of hounds and hares, and comfortable wingback chairs. Mom has also added interesting touches like lime-green lamps and exotic orchids. She even placed some fancy blue-and-white Wedgwood vases on the coffee tables—her new prized possessions. It doesn't sound like it should all work together, but somehow it does.

"Ah, I see someone's a botanist." Susan Klein peers at the art prints of ferns and other plants. "This is right up my alley."

"What do you do exactly?" I ask.

"As my son said, I'm a mycologist, which means I study fungi, including mushrooms," she says. "I'm helping research the environmental impacts of development that's slated for the area. I'm here to survey the forest nearby for diversity of fungi species."

"Oh, wow, that's so cool." I love exploring the woods nearby with Jules, and now a real, live forest scientist will stay at our bed-and-breakfast for a month. Maybe it won't be so bad after all to have long-term guests. I've also heard of the development that is being planned—the town wants to expand the downtown area to attract more tourists. Mom and Dad think it's a great idea as it'll bring more guests to our inn.

Max careens around the room, practically bouncing off the walls like a pinball. "These hares are the best. They're so cool standing on their hind legs like they're boxing each other. Who ever heard of boxing hares? If I had some hares, I'd train them to box for sure, and charge admission, and it'd be the biggest thing ever." He spreads out his arms, displaying an imaginary marquee. "Come see the Incredible Fighting Hares, a once-in-a-lifetime experience, only in the woods of Virginia."

My eyes widen and I lean away. I'm aghast—a new word I recently learned, which means horrified. *This* is the boy who will be living under the same roof as me for the next month? He's like a human version of Jules, except this boy talks and what comes out of his mouth is super strange. I do giggle silently at the idea of boxing hares.

Jules's barks echo from downstairs.

"Do you have a dog? I love dogs," Max says. "Can I meet your dog?"

His mother nods. "You can let your dog out," Susan says. "We love dogs."

My heart softens. Maybe these two aren't so bad if they're dog lovers like me. I go downstairs and release Jules, who runs up to say hello to them in a flurry of tail-wagging and wet kisses. "This is Jules."

Max bends down, holds out his hand to let Jules

sniff it, then tousles the fur on his head. "Hello, Jules. You're awesome. Amazing. So cool. I can tell we're going to be great friends." He ruffles the sheepadoodle's fur.

I press my lips together. This guy's awfully familiar with my dog. Jules wags his tail hard and tries to pounce on Max, but I pull him back. "No, Jules."

Jules and Max trade huge grins. The boy and my dog seem to have the same energy—both are exuberant and chaotic. It's overwhelming. I'm not sure I can handle another Jules, especially in person form.

"What kind of dog is he?" Max's mom asks. "I've never seen one like this before."

"He's a sheepadoodle, a mix between a sheepdog and a poodle," I explain. "My dad's allergic to dogs that shed, so Jules is perfect for him. It's also good for the inn, because some guests are allergic to dogs. We keep him mostly in our rooms or outside."

"That sounds like a smart idea."

"Here." I hand over the room keys. "We put you in the deluxe suite. It's an attachment to the main house with its own entrance. I'll take you there."

As we walk to the addition, Max says, "What do

you do for fun around here? Do you have hobbies?" He doesn't wait for an answer. "I saw you have some chickens out back. Can you show them to me? I can't wait to check out the whole property."

"Um, sure." Yikes. This mini storm of a person that's landed in our inn is a lot.

"Max, let's not bother Sienna now. After we get settled, I want you to come with me to the store to pick up some staples." Susan smiles as she looks around. "This is great. I could've tried to find a short-term rental for the summer, but this location is ideal for my research. Thank you, Sienna."

Max and his mom disappear into their rooms, and I sag against the porch column. I'm going to have to take vitamins to keep up with Max. When I return to our foyer, my eyes land on a water bottle covered with stickers—one is the strange design of the Maryland flag and another is a FIFA sticker. Max must've put it down and forgotten it when he greeted Jules. I place it on the table near the front door.

Finally, I'll have some time to check on the fawn.

My phone rings. I pull it out. It's my parents, on a video call. I flop onto the couch and answer.

CHAPTER FIVE

"Hi, Sienna, how are you?" Mom asks from the video call.

She and Dad are sitting on a wooden swing on a porch, their swaying making me slightly dizzy. They look relaxed for the first time in a long time—Mom wears her wavy brown hair down and a T-shirt and jeans, while Dad has on shorts and a tee. They're never this casual when they run the inn. I can see how everyone says I look just like my dad, with our dark, straight hair and wide cheekbones.

The muffin fire in the kitchen zips through my mind, but I don't want to ruin their mood. I remember Nainai's suggestion to tell them when they get back. "I'm okay. The new guests came." I explain how Dr. Klein is a scientist who studies mushrooms. "Her son is staying too."

"That's right," Mom says. "They're staying for a month. His school's done for the year, but they didn't figure out any summer programs for him. You should show him around and make him feel welcome at the inn."

I groan. "Do I have to?" Max is too much. Why can't he do his own thing? Besides, I'm too busy to babysit him, especially with Mom and Dad gone and Nainai now laid up with back pain. "Don't we usually say no kids at our inn?"

"We do," Dad says, "but we made an exception for Dr. Klein since she's staying for a month."

"When are you coming back?" It's nerve-racking to have all of the responsibility of the bed-and-breakfast on me. I wish my parents hadn't trusted me so much with the inn.

"On Sunday," Dad says. "Nainai tells us you're doing great running the morning chores."

I fidget. "I guess. How's your trip?"

Mom's brows furrow. "It's good, but we have a lot of work to do to match some of these other starred inns. We've got some big projects we could do to improve our bed-and-breakfast."

Dad scowls. "We don't need to make huge changes. A few special touches that add to the guest experience will be enough."

Mom shoots him a sharp look, then smiles brightly. "We'll tell you about our trip when we get back."

I sigh inwardly. I'm doing everything I can to help with the inn—special touches like folding towel animals and the fancy breakfast menus—but it sounds like we have to do even more. The dark looks Mom and Dad exchange with each other also worry me. I hate it when they fight, and it seems like they're doing it more and more. The fawn pushes into my thoughts. I almost tell them about it, but I don't have time to explain. "I should finish up my chores."

"Love you." Mom blows me a kiss and Dad waves.

I put down the phone and step outside, letting out a low whistle.

Jules trots over, his mouth a wide grin, tail wagging. I crouch down and pull him in—I need doggy love only Jules can deliver. He's such a sweetie; he leans in and licks my face. My heart immediately feels ten times lighter, like a balloon ready to fly.

"Let's go for a walk." We should check on the fawn.

Jules's ears prick up at one of his top three words. He sprints around the yard in a frenzied circle and back.

I laugh. "What a bundle of energy."

Jules trots by my side as we head to the long grass by the woods. He seems to know exactly what I want to do, because he makes a beeline to the spot where we last saw the fawn.

My heart catches in my throat. Part of me hopes the fawn's not there, because that would mean that it's safe with its mother somewhere else. The other part of me would love to see its cute little face again.

My heart squeezes when I see Jules nuzzling at a spot of brown in the grass. At the same time, I hear a *WEAH, WEAH*. It sounds like a cross between an angry baby and a toy car horn.

It's the fawn! It's sitting where we left it earlier, and it's crying. Surely, if the mother deer is around, she would've come by now and not ignored her baby's cries. A terrible thought comes over me—what if Mr. Buchanan set out poison and this fawn's mother ate it and died?

Jules goes over to the fawn.

I step closer, and the fawn yelps again.

Jules licks the deer on its head, which calms it down. The fawn looks up at Jules and nuzzles its head against him.

The fawn looks weak. Maybe it's injured.

Jules gives me pleading eyes, as if to say, *Can we help this fawn? It needs us.*

"Jules, I don't think I can take this fawn. It needs a doe mom, not a human one," I say. "We should leave it."

Jules circles the fawn and whines. He returns to me and wraps his front legs around my legs and lays his head against my side. This is his way of hugging me, but now it's more of a plea to help the small creature. Jules looks up with wide eyes and gives a small bark.

My shoulders sag. I really want to help the fawn, but I don't know anything about taking care of a little deer. I turn to the tiny animal. "You're so adorable. I wish I could help you, but I don't know how."

The fawn looks at me and puts its head down.

It makes me want to melt into a puddle and gather it up in a hug, but I should stay well away to not scare it. I drop to my haunches and put my arms around my dog. "Jules, what should we name this fawn?"

Jules leans against me.

I glance at the trees behind the fawn. One is a persimmon tree—a tall, stately tree with deeply grooved bark that grows one of my favorite pastry fruits. I smile. "I'll name you Persimmon. One day, you'll be as strong as this tree."

The little deer gives the sweetest look—Persimmon

seems to understand and approve of the name.

"Jules, come. Let's go." I head in the direction of the inn. "Want a treat?"

At the sound of his other favorite word, Jules's ears perk up. He licks Persimmon and nudges the fawn, as if reassuring it.

"Persimmon, I'll be back," I say. "I promise." I'll do some research to figure out how to help this fawn.

As we leave the field and are partway back to the inn, Jules turns and lets out a growl, low and extra fierce.

The hairs on my arms stand on end. I've never heard that sound come from my sheepadoodle before.

Jules barks urgently and runs back to the field and forest edge.

"Jules!" I chase after him.

There's a flash of brown at the edge of the woods. An animal that looks like a mean-looking dog with large, triangular ears and sharp teeth bursts out of the bushes.

A coyote!

My insides turn to mush. My heart pounds as if trying to leap out of my chest.

The coyote is about to pounce on Persimmon! The fawn is frozen in shock.

Jules runs faster than I've ever seen before, barking loudly, laser focused on the coyote. He reaches the predator before it can get to the fawn.

The coyote turns to Jules and bares its teeth. The two face and circle each other, both growling.

Jules is bigger than the coyote, but it lunges at my sheepadoodle.

Jules retreats briefly. But then he turns and runs back at the coyote. He barrels into the space between the fawn and the predator, barking and getting into the coyote's face.

The coyote runs away.

My heart is pounding.

It's gone.

But no—it runs back to Jules.

I hang back. I've never seen this kind of fight between animals. Everything seems to happen in slow motion.

Jules and the coyote go at each other, testing. They snap at each other, but I don't think their bites actually land. Jules keeps himself between the fawn and the coyote, and puts on a burst of speed, rushing at the coyote.

The coyote yips, turns on its heels, and runs back into the forest. Jules chases it into the trees. Now the coyote's really gone.

I run through the grass, heart hammering. Is Persimmon hurt? I reach the fawn.

Thank goodness—it seems okay.

I glance up. Jules runs back, and I gather him in my arms and give him the biggest hug. "Jules! You saved Persimmon's life!"

Jules, still riled up, wriggles out of my arms and goes to the fawn. He sniffs at it to make sure it's okay.

I let out a ragged breath. My body quivers with nervous energy at how close the coyote has come to us. Even though the animal was smaller than me, I'm shaken. I feel like I could've been its prey too.

Jules comes back and licks my face.

I crouch down and wonder what to do with the fawn. We can't leave it here with the coyote lurking in the woods. If that scavenger could scare me so much, I can only imagine what the poor fawn is feeling. "We have to get this fawn to safety."

CHAPTER SIX

I rack my brain. I have to get the fawn out of the field and somewhere safe. But I can't let my parents or Nainai know about Persimmon yet. They already have too much to worry about.

Plus, Dad is almost as bad as Mr. Buchanan about deer and will make me get rid of the fawn if he finds out. Not only does he complain about deer when they get into our roses, he's hated deer ever since he was bitten by a deer tick as a teen and got Lyme disease. I've grown up hearing about how I could get this dangerous infection from being outside and getting bitten by ticks. Even though the deer don't spread Lyme disease, they're one of the ticks' food sources. I don't know why he's like this, because Dad didn't even get seriously ill since they treated him in time.

I look toward the goat pen and my gaze lands on the storage shed next to it. That's it! Hardly anyone goes to the shed. It's the closest building to the woods and away from the house, so I'll be able to take the fawn there without being seen.

"Jules, stay here." With the coyote on the loose, I'm not going to leave the fawn alone for a single minute.

Jules circles Persimmon and sits by the fawn, taking his job seriously. Persimmon bleats a *weah* and bumps its head against Jules. My sheepadoodle noses the fawn and gives it a lick. The fawn looks at him with big, round, trusting eyes.

I run to the shed and grab a cardboard box and an old towel and bring them to Jules and the fawn.

Jules nudges the little animal, and Persimmon tries to get up. It doesn't look like anything is broken, but it isn't sturdy either. The fawn bleats a louder *WEAH*, and sticks its head under Jules's belly and nudges at him. It's trying to nurse from my dog.

"Poor thing, you must be hungry," I say. "Silly fawn, dogs won't give you milk. Plus, Jules is a boy. But I've got you—I'll take you somewhere safe and we'll get you fed." As I get closer, I tilt my head and look under the fawn. No male private parts; the fawn is a girl.

I bring the box close to the fawn and kneel by the little creature. "Hi, Persimmon. My name's Sienna. Your new friend is Jules."

Jules wags his tail and tries to prop the fawn up. The fawn sits back down. She seems weak or sick.

"Here we go." I use the towel to carefully wrap the fawn's little body to pick her up. *Okay, I've got this.*

I pick the fawn up, but Persimmon struggles, legs kicking. Even though Persimmon is tiny, she's stronger than she looks, so I have to tighten my grip and wrestle with the fawn.

"It's okay," I say gently. "I've got you."

Jules licks the fawn.

Persimmon quiets down.

I place the fawn carefully in the box and pile the towel around the tiny animal to try to keep her calm. Persimmon is heavier than I expect.

My heart pounding in my ears, I pick up the box and waddle toward the storage shed. The box grows heavier as I walk. Persimmon remains still; she's probably scared.

"Don't worry, cutie. Jules and I'll take care of you."

The fawn gives me a trusting look.

Inside the shed, I place the box in a corner. What a relief it is to put it down. The shed is warm, dry, and quiet—perfect for the little fawn to rest and recover. The inside is cluttered, with bags of feed on a pallet, buckets, and tools along one wall and a workbench along another. Bags of oats and garden supplies are stacked on a metal shelf.

Now I need to figure out how to feed Persimmon. She probably needs some kind of milk. Then I have an idea. The goat milk!

"Stay here," I tell Jules.

I run back to the inn to grab the milk I'd gotten earlier.

Nainai is wiping the counter, one hand rubbing her back. "Ready for lunch? I'll make you a sandwich." Her eyes twinkle. "Or cut you some perfect-sized pineapples."

I chuckle uneasily, trying not to look too guilty. "Maybe later. I'll finish cleaning up. How's your back? You should rest." I have to get Nainai out of the kitchen so I can grab the milk, transfer it into a feeding bottle, and warm it up for Persimmon. I hate hiding the fawn from my grandma and lying, but

Nainai won't understand. She dislikes deer as much as Dad does from his bout of Lyme disease, and I need to help the fawn now. Plus, Nainai *does* look like she needs to get off her feet.

My grandma's face transforms with her smile. "You're so sweet, Sienna. I'm improving, but you're right, I'll feel better lying down." She walks slowly out of the kitchen. It's so unlike her to be hampered like this; she usually bustles around the house doing three things at once.

Now I feel even worse, making Nainai think that my main concern is caring about her when I'm really lying to her. I glance at the dishes in the sink—they can wait until after I feed Persimmon. I dig through the storage room to find our old baby goat bottles.

Back at the shed, Persimmon cries out. The poor thing has to be so hungry.

I hurry over. "I'm sorry. I came as quickly as I could." I crouch down and bring the bottle to Persimmon's mouth. "I've got you some milk." I've helped my parents bottle-feed the baby goats, so I use the same tricks I know, dribbling some milk onto Persimmon's mouth.

The fawn moves her head away and bleats a sharp *WEAH*.

I sit back on my heels. It makes sense that the fawn isn't used to this strange plastic contraption, since the bottle isn't anything like her deer mom. A familiar tightness spreads through me. I have to convince Persimmon to drink something. If she doesn't soon, she probably won't survive.

Jules comes over and licks Persimmon, trying to calm her down.

"Please, just a sip." I push the bottle to Persimmon's mouth, but she rejects it again. "Why aren't you taking the milk? You have to be really hungry." Again, I try, and again, the fawn turns her head away.

Persimmon bleats again, this time more weakly.

My heart sinks. I thought the goat milk would be the answer. But, no—it's not enough.

I'm in over my head and have no one to turn to. I need to do some research on how to take care of a fawn. I can't let anything happen to Persimmon. If I don't get the fawn to drink something, she'll probably die.

I pull out my phone and search how to take care of a fawn. I learn that most fawns found alone are not abandoned by their moms, but if a fawn is in the same place for more than a day and a half and crying, it's likely that it has lost its mom. In fact, if a fawn is crying, it's a sign that it is extremely hungry.

I sit back. I have no idea how long she was in the field before we found her. She had definitely been crying and was in danger from the coyote. I couldn't have waited to see if the mother was around.

The advice online says to leave it to the experts to save a fawn. That's what I'll do: Find a wildlife rehabilitator to help me with Persimmon.

I search until I find a name and number of a woman nearby, Maite Santoja, who takes care of abandoned deer. I hate making calls, especially to strangers. But the little hungry fawn doesn't care about my fear of phones. I squeeze my eyes shut, take a deep breath, and make myself do it.

It rings several times, and it goes to a message explaining that Maite Santoja is out of town. Her voicemail is full so I can't leave my info.

"Now what?" I ask Jules.

Jules looks up from his spot standing guard, but gives me no answers.

"Let's go," I say. "We'll figure out something."

We leave the shed.

"Sienna, right?" It's Max, walking over with a friendly grin.

I close the door behind me and try to pretend everything is normal.

CHAPTER SEVEN

I turn to face Max. "Yeah, hi." I glance at the shed. I don't want to share Persimmon's existence with him. In fact, I'd rather not deal with him now at all, but Mom's request to be nice springs to mind. I give him a half-hearted smile.

Jules runs up to Max in a frenzy of doggy energy, wagging his tail and jumping on him.

"Hey, buddy," Max says.

"Down, Jules," I say. "No jumping."

Jules stops his pawing, but he doesn't rein in his excitement as he wiggles all over, letting Max pet him.

"Jules is awesome," Max says. "He's so fluffy and cute."

I find myself warming slightly to him. I trust Jules's instincts, so if he likes Max, maybe he's not a terrible person.

"What are you doing?" Max says, bouncing up and down on his heels.

"Checking on some supplies for the goats," I say

casually, even though my insides twist. I'm losing count of how many times I've lied this morning.

"Will you show me the woods?"

A walk in the woods would get my mind off Persimmon. *And I've been asked to babysit you.* "Okay. Mind if we take Jules? He could use a walk."

"Yeah, Jules is a cool dude of a dog."

I head back toward the inn.

"Aren't the woods the other way?" Max says.

"We'll need water. And some bug spray. Did you get your water bottle back?"

Max laughs. "I don't need a water bottle. It's not a trek into the wilderness. And a few bug bites never bothered me. I don't even notice them." He crouches into a fighting stance. "If the bugs come, I'll destroy them. Vanquish them. I'll be the harbinger of their doom!"

I raise an eyebrow. "There could be ticks in the woods, and you don't want to get bitten and get Lyme disease."

"Who gets Lyme disease?"

"Actually, my dad did. He got it when he was young and now he's super paranoid about ticks."

"Really? Is he okay now?"

"Yeah, but it's better to be prepared."

Max shrugs. "Fine, I'll spray chemicals on myself for the sake of your dad's childhood fears."

"We use organic oils that keep ticks away," I say. "Anyway, do whatever you want. I'm just trying to make sure our guests have an excellent experience at the Rolling Hills Bed & Breakfast."

"Well, in that case, hit me with those organic oils." Max grins. "I won't turn down an excellent experience at the Rolling Hills Bed & Breakfast!"

I can't help smiling. We go back to the inn to get the bug repellant and water, then walk back down to the trees. It makes me feel better to be prepared for anything. You never know when you might get dehydrated.

As we pass the shed, Jules runs over to it, barking.

I frown. Poor Persimmon's inside, alone and hungry. "Come back, Jules!"

"What's over there?"

"Not much." I force a smile. "Jules likes to hang out in the shed. It's like his playhouse."

"That's weird."

I'd rather he thinks we're weird than discover I'm hiding a fawn in our shed. I worry about Persimmon, but I don't know Max well enough to know how he'd react if I tell him about her.

Jules runs ahead into the trees. He sniffs at the plants and trees and leaves. *So many interesting smells!*

When we first moved here, I would sometimes get spooked by the forest, especially at the end of the day, when the dark, branchy arms loom overhead. Now the trees and their rustling leaves are comforting. I take in a deep breath of the cool air and some of the tension from the morning eases.

Max bounces from tree to tree.

Jules, excited by this, follows Max eagerly.

"You should be careful," I say. "There are gullies and dips where you could hurt yourself."

"Forests are the best." Max puts his hands on the bark of one tree, then runs to another, trailing his hands through low-hanging leaves. It's almost like he's playing tag with the trees.

Jules thinks it's a grand game and chases after him.

I laugh at his infectious energy. "Trees are pretty

cool," I say, "but they're kind of a blur of green leaves to me."

"Oh, no, there are so many different kinds of trees, and you can use their leaves to figure out what they are." Max picks up a branch that has fallen on the ground and shows me the rounded leaves. "These are from a white oak." He scuffles around until he finds a similar leaf, but more pointed. "And this is a red oak leaf."

"Cool." I've never paid much attention. I can tell leafy trees from pine trees, and can spot a maple leaf, but in the city there was no reason to pay special attention to trees.

Jules nuzzles at the leaves Max is holding.

Max grins. "Looks like he wants to let us know what he thinks about these leaves." He picks up another one. "Oh, this one's good. It's a tulip poplar leaf. It looks like a cat."

It's true. The leaf has two pointy tips that look like ears and two other wider tips that make up the face. I find another one, hold it up, and bounce it around in the air. "Meow!" I do my best cat imitation.

Jules's ears prick up and he barks.

Max and I giggle.

"So, what does your mom do in the forests?"

"She can tell you more," Max says, "but she studies how many fungi species are in the forest."

"Fungi, like mushrooms?" I say.

"Yeah, but fungi are a lot more than mushrooms."

"What do you mean?"

"The mushrooms are only the part you see above ground, and below there's so much more. And that part of the fungi is all over the place, especially in tree roots," Max says. "It's called mycorrhizal fungi." He hops off a log and joins me on the trail.

"Mike . . . oh . . . rye . . . ?"

"Mycorrhizae are fungi that live in the roots of the trees. They help keep the trees healthy by giving them more food."

"That's neat."

"If you think about it, in a way, trees are farming people," Max says.

"They what?" It sounds like we're unexpectedly in a horror movie.

"Think about it. They give us oxygen, and when we die, we decompose and go back to being food for the trees," Max says. "It's all part of their grand plan to colonize the planet."

"Eww. That's so morbid. I don't like thinking about that."

"It's just a way of thinking about it." Max laughs. "Don't worry, I'm sure these trees are your friends and don't have evil intentions."

I grin. "Whew. So they won't start poisoning us and breaking us down for mulch?"

Max holds up his hands in claws and walks like a zombie. "Beware the night of the living trees."

Jules circles, wagging his tail, the zombie walk a hit with him. *I like this funny guy,* he seems to say.

Max points to a tree we're walking by. "Okay, but this is what's cool about the fungi and mushrooms. See that large white oak tree? That could be a hub tree."

"A hub tree?"

"They're also called mother trees. They're older trees that help their relatives using the fungi living in their roots." Max's face lights up as he speaks. "They feed their baby trees."

"How do they do that?"

Max hops along some tree roots. "They can talk to each other."

"No way. Trees don't talk!" I'm beginning to think Max is making fun of me. I walk up to a tree and put my hand on the rough bark, then put my ear by it. "Hello? Are you saying something?"

Max laughs. "Not like that. Trees talk to each other through their roots, with the fungi." He spreads out his fingers and waves them. "Imagine all the roots and the fungi spreading out into smaller and smaller tendrils underground and they meet up with the fungi and roots of other trees."

My eyes widen. "More evidence that trees are like zombies."

"Like, if a tree is attacked by a bug, its fungi will send chemicals to other trees nearby, and the other trees will up their defenses."

"How?"

"The trees can make themselves more bitter or poisonous through their chemicals."

I stop, and my jaw falls open. "That's incredible." I've never thought about trees having needs or wants like other living things. It almost seems like the trees *care* for one another. I look up into the crowns above, the dappled light streaming through the leaves, and imagine the trees sharing their secrets.

I eye Max as he flits from tree to tree like a giant dragonfly. It's been a long time since I've had someone to hang out with like this. Since we moved from D.C., I haven't found a real friend yet, so it feels good to have this easy back-and-forth with Max. But I don't want to get too excited—I don't want to jinx myself. It still stings to remember my old bestie Cecilia telling me I'm too controlling. Maybe it's better to stick with Jules, who will never hurt me.

Jules follows Max, stopping every once in a while to poke his nose among leaves or into the dirt.

"What's this?" Max bends down to the area Jules is nosing and picks up something.

"Jules loves to find cool things." I take it and wipe the mud from the piece. "It's some kind of pottery or ceramic."

"Is it old? Is it valuable? Where's it from?"

"I don't know, but we have a book at the inn that'll tell us."

Max snatches the piece from me. "Oh, cool." He

dances around the leaves. "I bet this is super valuable and rare and treasure hunters will pay a huge bounty for it." His eyes shine and he shoves it too close to my face. "I'm going to be rich."

A prickle of annoyance goes through me. "Be careful with that." Max is so cavalier. In the short time I've known him, I can already tell that he doesn't take anything seriously. "And it's not yours to make money off of. Since it was on our property, it's the inn's."

Max laughs. "Ever heard of finders keepers?"

"In that case, it's Jules who found it." I knew I shouldn't have let my guard down with Max. "We'd better get back."

He shrugs and breaks into a grin. "I'm gonna believe that this *is* worth a fortune. I'm optimistic that way—glass-half-full kinda guy, and all."

I pick up my pace. *Glass half full of* something, I think.

He follows me. "Maybe I'll share my prize with you."

"Come on, Jules." I call him from Max's side. When Mom and Dad come home, I'll let them know they need to find someone else to make Max feel welcome.

CHAPTER EIGHT

Later in the day, I return to the shed to try to feed Persimmon again—but no luck. I sink my head into my hands. What if I'm doing it all wrong? I have no idea how long it's been since Persimmon has last eaten. Dread blooms in me. Maybe I can't save her.

I draw in a deep breath. I'll figure it out. I have to. I'll research, make a plan, and draw up lists and charts. Back at the inn, I find a notebook, wake the family laptop, and begin to research.

Based on her size and comparing her to photos, I guess that Persimmon is two or three weeks old. She's not a complete newborn that needs to be fed all the time, but she still needs milk two to three times a day. She should be drinking mostly milk but can nibble on grasses, weeds, and other plants soon. And . . . *whew!* Goat milk is the type of milk people use to save fawns.

Jules sneaks his head onto my lap, so I pet him as I read. I'll need to get some hay to soak up Persimmon's poop and pee and set out water for her too. I draw a chart in my notebook to list all the tasks I need to do and when. Making the chart makes me feel better, more in control.

I notice a tab open to the hotel review site we use. I click over and see two new reviews.

1/5 stars. A very disappointing stay. The innkeepers apparently rely on a child and an elderly person to keep it running, and unfortunately, the result was a kitchen fire and a sub-par breakfast. Do not recommend.

2/5 stars. The weekend started out dreamily. Rolling Hills Bed & Breakfast is a charming B&B in a beautiful, rustic location surrounded by woods and close to vineyards. We enjoyed our stay until this morning, when an incident at breakfast resulted in the fire department coming and kicking us out for half an hour. We cut our trip short to find another place to stay.

I feel like I've been kicked in the stomach. When Mom and Dad see these reviews, they're going to lose it. Having these bad reviews at the top of the page is terrible. No one's going to pay attention to all the other five-star reviews we've gotten. I close the tab and hope my parents won't think to look at the reviews for a while. When they do, I won't know how to explain the situation to them.

I get out my phone and try the rehabilitator again. Still no answer. And the same full voicemail.

Dinner with Nainai passes in a blur. I can't concentrate on our conversation or even enjoy Nainai's homemade dumplings, one of my favorite meals. I know this isn't fair to Nainai, who'd made them with love. All I can think of is Persimmon, sitting alone in the shed, getting hungrier and weaker. After dinner, I'll try again.

As we clear up after dinner, Nainai asks, "Want to watch some TV? We have some *Abbott Elementary* episodes to catch up on."

Persimmon's alone in the shed, hungry and cold. "I'm sorry, Nainai, I have homework."

Nainai's eyebrows shoot up. "You've never been so diligent about school that you volunteered to do it over TV time. Isn't it almost the end of the year?"

"Nainai"—I force a smile—"are you trying to make me *not* do my work? I'm shocked!"

My grandma chuckles. "No, go and be a good student. I'll watch my own show." She heads to the sitting room where she'll watch her C-drama while knitting. Sometimes she really gets going and has the Weather

Channel on TV while simultaneously watching her show on a tablet and knitting.

I feel bad putting off my grandma, but I have to try again with Persimmon. It's Sunday and tomorrow's a school day. If I don't get Persimmon to eat tonight, she might not last the night. I grab the bottle of milk I stashed earlier in the storage room and run it under hot water in the kitchen sink to warm it up.

I open the kitchen door. Jules comes over eagerly, as if he knows exactly where I'm heading.

At the sound of the creak, Nainai leans over. "Where are you going?"

My heart pounds as I angle my body away to hide the bottle in my hand. "I'm . . . going to take some photos of the goats. It's for a school project."

Nainai looks at me quizzically. "That's homework?"

I smile ruefully. "It's an art project. It's more atmospheric to take sunset photos than middle-of-the-day ones." My mouth is dry. I hate telling lies, but if Nainai finds out about Persimmon, she'll make me return her to the woods.

"How fancy! Back in my day, we made paintings with macaroni and beads." Nainai chuckles and turns back to her show. "Okay, but don't stay out too long."

"I won't." I step out of the room and my shoulders slump in relief.

Jules and I hurry out to the shed. Persimmon is still tucked in the cardboard box where I left her in the corner. Jules goes over, and he and Persimmon greet each other like longtime friends, licking and nuzzling each other.

At the sight, I feel lighter. Jules is such a good friend to Persimmon. My attempt to get the fawn to drink *has* to work this time.

I tip the bottle and dribble some milk onto the fawn's mouth. At the taste of the sweet milk, Persimmon gives a tentative slurp, then stops.

"You can do it." I offer the bottle again, this time pushing and pulling the bottle, and repeating it, until finally, Persimmon catches on. The fawn pulls at the bottle. I hold the bottle up above her, and—success!—Persimmon gulps down the milk. "Yeah!" Joy surges through me as Persimmon drinks the lifesaving milk.

The little creature will be okay!

As Persimmon drinks, I look her over carefully. The fawn looks very thin—I can see her ribs—but otherwise okay, with clear eyes and no injuries.

Jules sits by Persimmon's side as she gulps down the milk, clearly super hungry. When she's done, the fawn seems sleepy. Jules licks Persimmon and settles down next to her, his tail wagging from side to side.

I sag in relief. "Jules, you have a new friend now."

Jules snuggles next to the fawn, and Persimmon rubs her head against his. They lie next to each other, the cutest sight I've ever seen.

In that moment, the heavy responsibility presses down on me. This little creature depends on me; in fact, her very life is in my hands. I blink rapidly from the weight of that thought.

I take a deep breath. I'm not sure I'm doing the right thing, but Persimmon seems to be doing okay, especially with Jules keeping her company and being her friend. I can do this.

"Jules, let's let Persimmon rest."

When I get back to my room, I collapse onto my bed, with no energy left to do my homework. But I don't care.

I've saved Persimmon.

CHAPTER NINE

The next morning, before school, I sneak out to the shed to feed Persimmon. This time, Persimmon lets me approach her and give her the bottle. She slurps the milk like an expert. What a smart little thing.

I sigh and rub my temple. I hate leaving Persimmon just as I've gotten her to start drinking milk, but I have to go to school. Nainai told me I didn't have to do as much for breakfast today because of school, but it's not fair for my grandma to do all the work, especially with her back still hurting. So I woke up extra early to help her. My parents have really left us in the lurch.

Getting through the school day is tough, because I'm so distracted thinking about the fawn. Plus, I can barely keep my eyes open. When Ms. DeGaetani asks me to name the object in the solar system that was demoted from being a planet, I answer absentmindedly, "Persimmon."

The class whoops and hollers and I want to sink

through the floor. I try to make myself small and refuse to look up for the rest of the class. It's bad enough that I don't have any friends at school, but now I'll be labeled the weirdo for the rest of the year.

When I get home, I feel better after sitting with Nainai and snacking on grapes and cheese. I put my head down for a minute to rest my eyes.

"Are you okay? You're looking very tired," Nainai says. "Staying up late watching those survival videos again? I swear, I don't know where you pick up your hobbies."

"It's not that." Because I worry about lots of things, I like watching videos on dealing with unexpected situations. I just learned, for example, that if I'm attacked by bears, I should fight black bears but play dead with grizzly ones. But of course, that's not what's on my mind now. "I didn't sleep well last night."

"You're just like me." My grandma turns serious. "You're too young to be losing sleep over worries. What's going on?"

I'm tempted to blurt it all out. It'd be such a relief to confide in my grandma about Persimmon, but I have to make sure the fawn is okay before I tell anyone about her. If I can show my parents and Nainai that I can take care of Persimmon, then maybe they'll let me keep her. The bad reviews also weigh on my mind. "It's just some school stuff."

"Want to talk about it?"

I'm grateful for her concern, but I shake my head. "I'll figure it out."

"I noticed Jules spent a lot of time behind the goat pen today, whining at the shed," Nainai says. "I didn't go down to check because of my back. Maybe there are mice or something there. Can you check it out?"

Yikes, she might be getting suspicious. "I'm sure it's nothing, but yeah, I'll go." I wish I could speak sheepadoodle, because I need to let Jules know that he's blowing our secret.

Nainai and I share a hug before I head outside. I love the scent of pastries and coffee that comes off her apron.

At the shed, Jules lies by the door outside. He leaps to his feet and barks excitedly. "Jules, you're doing a great job guarding Persimmon, but you can't be so obvious about it."

Jules wags his tail and smiles. *I have no idea what*

you're saying, human. I just want to play with Persimmon, he seems to be telling me.

Once inside, I gasp. The cardboard box that was holding Persimmon is empty. I rush in to look for the fawn.

A quick scan around the interior.

No Persimmon.

My knees go wobbly. I hadn't thought to pen Persimmon into a smaller area because she was so weak and hadn't moved from her box. But obviously I was wrong and she's wandered off. She could be hurt somewhere in the shed. Or maybe she's escaped somehow.

Jules dashes over to a corner behind some bags of goat feed and makes snuffling sounds.

I follow him and take a sharp breath. Persimmon is curled up in a corner, tucked under a bunch of rakes and other tools. They're balanced like pick-up sticks, about to topple any minute.

Persimmon looks at Jules and bleats a small *weah*.

Jules nudges his nose into the pile of tools and they shift.

"No, Jules!" I run to catch the tools, wincing as they clatter.

I catch a rake just before it slams on Persimmon and stick my hand and part of my shoulder above the fawn to shield her from the rest of the falling tools. I yelp as they fall around me, glancing off my back and arm. They hurt.

I clear the tools out of the way, rubbing my sore arm, and Jules comes over to Persimmon. At least she's okay, but the poor fawn is probably scared out of her mind. Persimmon looks up at Jules, stands up, and toddles after him.

"Come on, Jules," I say, "let's get Persimmon back to her box."

Jules follows my lead, and Persimmon comes after Jules.

I search for something to use as a barrier to pen Persimmon into the corner. I drag bags of goat feed and make a wall. I plop down on one and deflate like a week-old balloon.

I tried to do everything but had forgotten the most basic thing—to keep Persimmon safe. *Think.* I need a better solution than a wall of bags.

Then I remember. The puppy pen. When we first got Jules as a puppy and were training him, we'd set up a pen made out of plastic fencing. It'd be perfect for Persimmon. It's in the storage room off the kitchen.

"Jules, will you stay here and take care of Persimmon?"

Jules is already by Persimmon's side, licking her fur, and Persimmon seems to enjoy this attention. *Of course, this fawn is the best,* Jules seems to say.

Persimmon stands up and walks around the cramped space, Jules following attentively like her own personal bodyguard. I glance around to make sure there aren't any other obvious dangers.

"Jules, keep her safe."

Jules seems to know what to do as he steers the fawn away from the corner where the tools lie in a jumble.

I slip out of the shed and hurry to the house. Back at the inn, Nainai is upstairs cleaning one of the guest rooms. That's lucky for me, because now I can sneak to the storage room for Jules's old pen.

The room holds old filing cabinets, plastic containers, racks of wine, boxes, and more. And there it is: In a corner, under a tarp, I find the parts of the old puppy pen. They're light and will lock together easily, but I'll need to make several trips.

I collect a couple segments and head out the kitchen door, keeping an ear out for my grandma. On the third trip, I step out of the storage room with the two last pieces I need . . . and jump.

Nainai stands in front of me holding a basket of sheets. "What in the world are you doing?"

"Um . . ." I have to come up with something quickly, but I'm not used to lying to Nainai. "I thought it would be, um, fun to set up Jules's old pen and play with him in it."

Nainai's puzzled look says, *Is the early summer heat getting to you?* "Mmm. Don't you have all that homework?"

My mouth goes dry and I swallow. I totally do have a ton of homework. "I don't have that much."

"Well, have fun," Nainai says, transferring the sheets into the washing machine and shaking her head.

I hustle out and just in time. Persimmon is exploring the shed, but Jules stands protectively close. "Thank you, Jules."

Before long, I've put the pieces together and set up a pen in the corner of the shed. I hold open the gate. "Here, Jules!"

He trots over and comes into the pen, sniffing

around, probably remembering it from his puppy days.

Persimmon follows him into the space, and the two of them circle the area, their tails wagging in unison.

I lay back on the pile of feed bags, and let out a long sigh.

All I have to do now is repeat what I did today for the rest of the week: Get up extra early to check on and feed Persimmon, take care of the chickens and goats, and help with breakfast, all while keeping the fawn's existence from Nainai. And somehow not fall over in an exhausted heap at the end of each day.

CHAPTER TEN

It works for almost two days: I get up. Help Nainai with breakfast. Take Jules out while I milk the goats and gather eggs. Sneak down to the shed to feed Persimmon. Watch Jules and Persimmon play for fifteen minutes and drag them apart as they try desperately to stay together longer. Hop on the bus. Almost fall asleep in school. Come back home and sneak back to the shed. Play with Jules. Do some homework. Help Nainai with the inn and dinner.

It's Wednesday, and I wonder how much longer I can keep this up. I hop off the bus and head straight to the shed. Jules, waiting by the door, leaps to his feet and runs over to me.

I kneel down and give him a huge hug.

"Sienna!"

Max jogs up to me. "What are you doing? Can I join you? Why's Jules always hanging out here?"

Eek. I want to get to Persimmon, and my mind's a blank. "Um . . ." I stare at him. It'd be a huge relief to share my secret with someone. But can he keep a secret?

"It looks like you're trying to decide whether to trust me or not with something," Max says.

I twist my lips. He's not a bad mind reader.

"You can. You know why?" He picks up a stick and holds it in the air like a sword with one hand and stands in a triumphant pose with his other hand on his hip. "Because I am a trustworthy person. You can rely on me."

I smile despite myself. He's so over-the-top, but him being silly and funny makes me almost like him. Or maybe I'm just too tired to think straight. Plus, Persimmon is so adorable, it's not fair to keep her completely hidden from everyone. "Okay, I do have something to share, but you have to promise not to tell anyone."

Max's eyes widen. "Of course, I promise. I love secrets. You'd be surprised by how many secrets I've kept. Even my secrets have secrets. I am the best secret-keeper ever."

I snort. "You don't have to be the best secret-keeper, just a pretty good one."

"I can do that," Max says. "Actually, I don't have *that* many secrets. I'm not the sneaky sort."

"I didn't really think you were." I'm beginning to get that Max sometimes says things just for the effect and not because he believes what he says.

"Are you hiding something in there?" Max's face lights up. "I know! You're a mad plant scientist and you've created a carnivorous plant that will eat little children. I want in on your devious plan to rule the world. We'll name him Seymour."

"No." I snort. "Where do you get your weird ideas?"

"One person's weird is another's genius."

I roll my eyes. "Whatever." I open the door. "Anyway, be quiet. You don't want to scare her."

"Her?"

As we step inside, I let my eyes adjust to the dim interior.

"Meet Persimmon."

Persimmon is curled up in her box, a small ball of a fawn. Jules greets Max, his tail in overdrive.

Max's brows shoot up and his jaw drops. A smile races across his face and he's about to rush over to Persimmon, but I hold him back.

"It's a fawn!" he says in a soft, delighted voice. He turns to me. "What's it doing here?"

"I found her over the weekend." I explain how Jules found Persimmon and saved her from the coyote.

"How do you know her mom isn't around?" Max asks.

"I don't know for sure, but she was crying from hunger and we had to get her away from the coyote," I say. "I think my neighbor might've done something to the mom, like poisoned her."

Max's expression is one of pure horror. "Why would he do that?"

"He hates the deer that come into his garden. It's horrible."

"Wow. No wonder you're hiding the fawn in here."

"It's not just my neighbor. I don't want my parents or grandma to know about Persimmon yet."

"Why not?"

I scrunch my brows together. It's hard to explain. "I want to take care of Persimmon and help her. It'd be great to keep her, because I love her so much already, but my dad hates deer, and I'm sure my mom thinks I have enough to do with Jules and the chores around the inn."

"Well, I'm glad you told me about Persimmon. She's awesome."

Relief washes over me. He gets me and doesn't judge. Maybe I was wrong about my first impression of him.

Max scrunches down by the pen and peers at the fawn, and looks up again. "I've got a great idea."

I'm not sure I want to hear it. "What?"

"I'll help you."

"With what?"

"With taking care of Persimmon. During the day, I can keep an eye on her and help feed her and stuff until you're out of school too."

I purse my lips. My immediate reaction is no. When I decided to show him Persimmon, I didn't mean for him to horn in on what I'm doing. I've been taking care of her, and she's been doing fine.

But then, the weariness of the past few days settles in my bones. I've been barely holding it together. Persimmon could've gotten hurt in the shed because I'd missed something so basic as penning her in. And Jules spends all day sitting outside the shed pining for the fawn. Maybe Max *can* help with her. If Max is around during the day, Jules and Persimmon could see each other more.

But I wonder if Max can take care of the fawn. He seems too excitable and scattered to be reliable. Even now, he's got his fingers in his ears and he's waggling them at Persimmon while hopping from one foot to another.

Persimmon looks at him curiously, her little tail wagging. Jules stands by her with his tongue lolling out. Both of them seem mesmerized by his antics. Maybe he could be a help.

"Really?" I say tentatively.

"Yeah, how hard could it be?" Max says. "You have a dog, and that's a lot more work. It doesn't seem like you need to walk the fawn or anything."

I frown. "It's not that easy. I've been researching, and there's a lot involved with taking care of a fawn. We have to feed her, help her poop, keep her area clean, and . . ."

But Max isn't listening. He's gone into the pen and crouches next to Jules and the fawn. "Hello, little deer. How are you? I'm so glad to meet you, Persimmon. I'm going to take care of you. We're going to have so much fun."

Jules inserts himself between Max and Persimmon, as if guarding her from this excitable human. Jules even pushes Max away from the fawn with his head.

Persimmon doesn't seem too fazed by Max, but sticks close to Jules.

"Come away," I say. "You'll scare her."

Max joins me back outside the pen. "So, what do we need to do? Tell me all about taking care of her."

"We need to feed her at least twice a day with goat milk," I say. "I get hay from the barn for the floor."

As I speak, Max walks around the shed and peers at everything in it. He opens the flaps of boxes and checks out the various bins of feed and fertilizer.

I wince at the noise he's making. "Can you walk around more gently? Persimmon is a delicate creature. Are you even listening?" Confiding in Max might be a terrible idea. "I have a chart with everything we need to do."

Jules barks, and we look over at Persimmon. The fawn has retreated to a corner and curled up in a ball. Jules stands in front of her to give her cover.

Max's eyes widen. "Is she okay?"

"I think so," I say. "She's probably overwhelmed with both of us here. Let's give her some space and quiet."

As we ease toward the door, Jules licks Persimmon, and she nuzzles him back.

"Jules, you're such a good friend to Persimmon."

Jules gives me a look, as if to say, *I'm your friend too, but this little one needs me more now.*

"I'll show you how I milk the goats, and then we can feed her."

We slip out while Jules and Persimmon settle down next to each other. For the moment, I feel better. Persimmon has Jules to keep her company and I've shared my burden with Max, even though it feels a lot like handing a basket of eggs to a toddler.

CHAPTER ELEVEN

Almost immediately, I regret letting Max help take care of Persimmon. On Thursday, when I get home from school, I rush out to the shed to check on her. Jules stands protectively over Persimmon, while Max watches them both from outside the enclosure. Persimmon is chewing on dandelions and clover.

"Why did you feed her these plants without checking with me?" I say.

"Why do I have to check in with you? You're not my boss."

So many reasons rush to mind. Because they could've harmed her. Because Max could've done it wrong. "Did you go through the checklist?"

"No, I just made sure she was happy and fed," Max says. "You know, as long as the vibes are good."

I go bug-eyed. "The *vibes*?" I really shouldn't have let Max help me.

"Listen, she's fine. Look how much she loves it."

I have to admit it. Persimmon is chomping on

those weeds like they're gourmet deer food. I press my lips together. "Okay, but did you feed her some milk too?"

"I did, about eleven in the morning."

"That's not the schedule I made out."

"Schedule, schmedule," Max says. "Persimmon's a living soul. She's growing, and she wants milk when she wants it."

"It's better if we keep her on a schedule." It feels like I'm on a sled and Max has pushed me careening down a hill.

On Friday, I head to the shed, wondering what I'll find. I pick up the pace. I'm still not used to leaving important things to someone else. Can I really trust Max's vibes to take care of Persimmon? I fling the door open.

Inside the shed, Max is crouched by the pen, where Persimmon and Jules are playing.

Jules comes up to Persimmon, nudges her with his nose, and retreats. The fawn jumps and dances around my sheepadoodle, as frisky as can be. Then it's her turn to poke her head at Jules and edge away play-fully. Persimmon leans back, stretching out her front limbs and wiggling her backside, like she's taunting him. The two chase each other in a circle. They're having the best time.

"How's it going?" I ask.

Max smiles. "She's doing great—she drank her milk, and now look at them. I even milked one of your goats myself to give her fresh milk."

"What?" I've shown him how to do it, but I'm sure he won't have remembered all the steps. "Did you disinfect your hands before milking? Did you use the goat milking stand properly? Clean the udders?" My mind races at all the things he's sure to have done wrong.

"Yeah, I did all that." Max looks annoyed. "You showed all that to me; I knew what I was doing."

"Did you put everything away?"

A look of concern crosses his face. "I think so?"

"Max! There's a process to doing things properly. You can't just wing it."

"I'm sorry, I'll go back and clean up." Max looks over at Persimmon. "You know, I think Persimmon's ready to go outside. She's so much more active now."

I frown. "We can't let her out. She's still too young,

and my parents can't know she's here. If she's outside, we won't be able to hide her."

"Your parents aren't here now," Max says. "Why don't we let her out and keep her behind the shed, close to the woods? No one will be able to see her from the house."

"It's not going to work," I say. "She'll run off." Even though Max is a help, he's so presumptuous making decisions about Persimmon. She isn't *his* fawn.

"Just saying, you can't keep her here forever," Max says. "This fawn needs some sunshine and a place to run around."

"But she's still young. We have to keep her protected." My procedures and plans have kept her safe. We don't need to change what's working.

I need to get away from him. Max is so frustrating, doing things his way, ingratiating himself with *my* Persimmon. "I'm going back to the house. Come on, Jules." I open the pen to let Jules out.

Persimmon follows close at his heels, a yearning expression on her face, as if she'd follow her bestie anywhere. She nudges and headbutts the pen, causing the plastic walls to shake.

"See what I mean?" Max says.

"I'm sorry, Persimmon." I close the pen. "You've got to stay. I promise we'll be back soon."

Jules gives me a pleading look: *Can Persimmon come out and play?*

"Not you too." They're ganging up on me, three against one, but I need to stay firm in my decision not to let Persimmon out.

Max kneels by the fawn and she lets him give her a little tickle on her chin. "I'll hang out for a bit more," he says.

A pang stabs me in the heart. What if Persimmon's bonding with him more than with me? I let out a huff and storm out of the shed.

I head back up to the inn.

And stop short at the scrumptious smell of garlic frying in olive oil.

My father turns from the kitchen stove and smiles. "Hi, Sienna."

I grin at the sight of Dad, but my stomach does a couple of flips. "You're back early." Mom and Dad aren't supposed to be back until Sunday. I was going to cover up my tracks with Persimmon, like hide the bottles of goat milk that are in the storage fridge, and now it's too late.

Dad sets down the spatula, and we exchange a big hug. "Good to see you, Bug."

I snuggle into his arms. It's great to have him and Mom back. I can already feel the burden of my responsibilities lifting. "Where's Mom?"

"She's out with the goats," he says. "Nainai said they aren't giving as much milk this week."

I pull back and gulp. I didn't think Nainai would notice the missing milk I'd been giving Persimmon. "They seem fine to me. Maybe it's something in their food or the weather." I change the topic. "How were the places you visited?"

Dad shrugs. "They were fine."

"Did you get any good ideas?"

"Some. There are only so many ideas we can get from others. We're doing okay. We just need to be in tip-top shape when the accreditors from the Star Innkeepers visit."

"When's that?"

"We don't know. They gave us a window of the next ten days. It'll be a surprise visit; they want to know the inn is up to standards anytime someone drops by."

"Like a pop quiz."

"Exactly."

Ugh. Now I have to worry about strangers stopping by at any moment to judge our family's livelihood. "What are you making?"

"Lasagna."

At the barn, Mom is filling the trough with hay. Her face lights up when she sees me. She puts down the hay fork and comes in for a hug. "Hi there, sweetie."

I return her hug extra hard. "I'm glad you're back." I really am. Besides having her around, I'll have fewer things to worry about.

Mom looks at Cocoa, one of the milking goats. "Nainai said the goats are giving less milk, but when I checked, they seemed to be fine." Her brows knit together. "No sign of sickness."

I don't say anything.

"But look at Butterscotch. She doesn't look well." Mom kneels down by one of the other goats and feels her side.

Butterscotch is sitting in the corner while the other goats are eating. The goats never miss a chance at food, so something's wrong if she's ignoring the hay.

"We should call Dr. Walling. Maybe there's something going around," Mom says.

My insides squeeze together. What if Persimmon carries a disease and she's unknowingly infected Butterscotch? I've been careful to wash my hands before and after taking care of Persimmon and the goats, but it isn't easy to be perfect all the time. I don't want Mom to call the vet, because a vet might figure out there's a new animal in the picture. "I'll bring her some water. Maybe she's dehydrated." I hope with all my might this is all that's going on and the goat isn't really ill.

An even worse thought comes to mind. If it's possible for Persimmon to get the goats ill, then she could also accidentally get Jules sick. He's my best friend in the world, and I would never forgive myself if Jules got sick because of something I've done. All he wants to do is play with his new best friend, but what if that friend ends up hurting him, or even worse?

"You're brooding," Mom says. "Don't worry about Butterscotch. I'm sure she'll be fine."

"I'm sorry I didn't notice she wasn't well."

"It's okay; I'm more concerned with the drop-off in milk from the goats," Mom says. "Usually, a goat will produce as much milk as is needed. If there's more demand for milk, the goat will produce more. If we're milking the same amount every day, it shouldn't go down."

"Doesn't the milk go down over the season?" I hope this will be a good enough explanation to allay Mom's worries.

"It's still early. At this time of the year, the goats should still be making plenty of milk." She frowns. "Speaking of milking, you left a mess in the barn. I had to wash the collection bucket and put away the supplies. It's very unlike you to be so sloppy."

A dark cloud forms inside me. Max left everything a mess, and now I have to take the blame for him. It's so maddening to not be able to defend myself. I swallow my bitter thoughts. "I'm sorry, I had a late start and almost missed the bus. I was going to get back to this." I mentally add this to all the things I'm going to yell at Max about.

What Mom said gets me thinking. If goats can

make more milk with more demand, maybe I should just milk more on top of what I usually do. "I know you're back now, but I'd like to keep milking the goats."

Mom glances at me and raises an eyebrow. "Really? Can you handle it?"

"I can. I'm sorry about the mess up."

"Well, it would be a help. We've got a lot of planning to do for upgrades around here. You're really stepping up, Sienna."

I sigh inwardly. I'm only offering to do this to help Persimmon. In reality, adding goat milking to my chores may be too much, but I can't share that with Mom.

As we tidy the feeding area, Mom says, "I hear you've been hanging out with the boy who's staying with us. That's great."

"I suppose." I wish I could confide in her and tell her all about how frustrating Max is for doing things in ways we haven't agreed to, and how he's making me look bad. "Sometimes he's a bit much though."

"What do you mean?"

"He's just a lot, especially when he gets excited. He can be all over the place."

"Does that make you uncomfortable?" Mom asks.

I think about it. Max is so different from me. He's like a tornado when I'd rather hang out with a gentle breeze. "No, but he gets on my nerves."

Mom smiles. "Well, sometimes people say that about me. People can rub each other the wrong way, but if they're kind and honest, they can be worth being friends with."

I think about Max—his heart is in the right place, but his methods seem designed for maximum annoyance.

"I'm going to invite him and his mom to join us for dinner tomorrow," she says. "Let's make an effort to be friendly, okay?"

"Fine." If only she knew how much of an effort I make every day to hold myself back when I'm with him. I do need his help with Persimmon, so I'll do my best.

CHAPTER TWELVE

"Thanks so much for having us for dinner," Max's mother says as she adds salad to her plate.

We sit around the dining room table. Everyone's here, except Nainai, who's resting in her room.

"So, tell us about your work," Mom says. "Have you been settling in? What're you working on?"

"I'm studying the variety and number of mushrooms in the forests near where the development is slated," Dr. Klein says.

"Why are you doing that?" Dad asks.

"It tells us the health of the forests," Dr. Klein explains. "The builders of the new project need to look at its environmental impacts."

"So, your research could stop the proposal to expand downtown if it'll hurt the forest?" Dad asks.

"It doesn't usually get that far," Max's mom says. "If there are serious impacts, the government might require changes to how they go forward."

"But it'll make the project more difficult," Mom

says. "I hope you don't find anything to stop the expansion. We could use more people coming to this area."

Max's mom laughs. "It's not up to me. I just do the research and write a report."

I'm uneasy at Mom's words. I thought part of the appeal of our inn was that it's in a wild location and not because it's close to civilization. "Max was telling me about the micho . . . something network?" I say. "About how trees talk to each other through their roots?"

Max's mom nods. "Yes, something like that. Almost all plants and trees have extensive fungi in their roots; they look like white tendrils. They're called mycorrhizae and it's a symbiotic relationship, which means they depend on each other. The fungi give trees water and nutrients, and the trees give back sugars and carbon."

"What does that have to do with how trees talk to each other?" Dad asks.

"Scientists have shown trees use their root networks to help other trees nearby, like sharing food with their offspring trees, or sending chemical signals letting other trees know of an insect attack," Dr. Klein says.

"What do mushrooms have to do with it?" Mom asks.

"Mushrooms are the fruit of the fungi—the part that you see and people eat," Max's mom explains. "So the more types of mushrooms we find aboveground, the more complex and productive the underground network is, and therefore, the healthier the forest."

"They've called this network 'the wood wide web,'" Max says.

I smile. The idea of an underground tree network is pretty awesome.

Dr. Klein adds, "There's scientific debate about whether there's a cooperative network among trees. Some scientists believe it's too simplistic to say trees help each other, when many times they compete against each other. But I think it's a matter of how we talk about it."

"What do you mean?" I ask.

"Well, trees exchange information and chemicals," she explains. "Some people say that means trees 'talk' to each other, while others say that's just a natural process. Critics don't like it when we give too many human qualities to trees."

"Gotcha," Mom says. "You say *potahto*, I say *potayto*."

Dr. Klein smiles. "Something like that." She turns to me and Max. "Do you kids want to join me tomorrow to see my research site?"

I sit up. Max is a pain when it comes to taking care of Persimmon, but I'll put up with him to learn more about the trees. For some reason, when his mom talks about trees and how they connect with one another, it plucks at something in me. It makes me want to visit the trees to see for myself. "I'd love that." I turn to my parents. "Can I go?"

"We have a lot to do at the inn." Dad gives me a pointed look.

I'm sure he's reminding me of my promise to help him out. I slump in my chair.

Mom leans in. "It sounds fun. You should do it."

I shoot her a grateful look. "Do you also study other forest things besides fungi?" I ask Max's mom. "Animals, like deer, for example?" Persimmon's top of my mind. I wonder how the fawn's family is doing out in the woods.

"Not directly."

Dad rolls his eyes. "Deer are a nuisance. They're overrunning our forests, coming into our yards, and getting hit by cars. They're a menace to people and themselves."

"You sound like Mr. Buchanan," I say. "I'm afraid he might be poisoning the deer."

"What makes you say that?" Mom says sharply.

"Something he said the other day."

"I doubt that's what's happening," Mom replies. "We should ask him."

"It might not be a bad idea," Dad muses, "as long as it's legal."

"Dad!" I say. "It's *not* legal."

"I'm kidding," Dad says. "It's just that deer don't have any natural predators around here, and they're attracted to farms and gardens because they're easy pickings compared to foraging in the forest."

I think about the coyote that wanted to attack Persimmon. Maybe the adult deer don't have predators, but poor Persimmon certainly does. "Deer don't even bother our gardens," I say. "Jules keeps them away, so why do you care?"

"Jules isn't always outside," Dad says.

"Actually, I feel bad for the deer," Mom says. "Deer coming close to where people live is dangerous for them. The other day, on our way out to visit other inns, we saw a deer on the side of the road that had been hit."

A chill goes down my back, and I put down my fork. Maybe the deer they saw was Persimmon's mom, and that's why she's an orphan. An even more horrible thought strikes me. If Persimmon gets out of the shed, she could get hit by a car too. I feel sick to my stomach.

"I don't know a lot about deer," Dr. Klein says, "but they're part of the forest ecosystem. In a healthy forest, deer help clear the underbrush without over-eating the plants." Her expression grows serious. "But oaks are dying in our area, and oak leaves and acorns are one of deer's favorite foods. As they run out of food in the forest, deer come to people's neighborhoods and eat their gardens and rosebushes."

"Why are the oaks dying?" Dad asks.

"Different reasons. Many of the oaks are getting old now, and climate change and development affect them," Max's mom says.

"The best thing about deer is they're really cute, especially the fawns," Max says.

I kick him under the table. I don't want our parents to wonder how he knows they're cute.

Max shoots me a glare.

His mother looks at him quizzically. "I suppose so."

"And they love to be outside, right?" Max says. "Like, they shouldn't be kept in cages."

I glare daggers at him. It's almost like he's trying to get us caught.

"Of course," his mom says.

I want to hear more about how trees talk to one another, but it's too risky staying when Max seems to want to give away our secrets. I lean over and say under my breath, "Let's get out of here."

Max glances at the adults and nods. We ask to be excused.

Outside, Max and I head to the shed. Jules immediately follows us, ready to play with his bestie. I round on Max. "What is wrong with you?"

His eyes go round, but his fake look of surprise doesn't fool me. "What do you mean?"

"Why were you practically telling everyone about Persimmon?"

"I wasn't going to give away anything. Didn't you

notice how sneaky I was when I asked about fawns?"

"No, I only noticed how obvious and suspicious you sounded."

Max holds up his hands. "Don't get so worked up. It's not that serious."

"But it *is* serious." I take a deep breath. I'm going to stop arguing, because I've made my point and Persimmon needs us. "Let's figure out how to sneak into the kitchen, get the goat milk from the fridge, warm it up, and get it to Persimmon without anyone noticing." I lean in close. "Here's what we need to do. You go in and sit back down and get them really involved in a conversation. You can talk about trees and mushrooms, but not deer. Then I sneak in."

Max shakes his head. "That's too complicated, Miss Bossypants. The adults aren't paying attention to us. Let's just go get the milk, and if they ask, we say whatever's on our mind."

"That leaves everything to chance," I complain.

"You worry too much," he says. "Will you try it my way? Come on, live a little." Max smiles in a teasing way.

For the thousandth time this week, I wonder why I let Max help me with Persimmon. But I admit he hasn't actually hurt her. He might have a point that it's simpler to get the milk without a complicated plan. "Okay," I say.

It turns out that Max is right. Our parents don't even notice when we get the milk and slip out of the kitchen. Jules runs over and joins us as soon as he realizes where we're heading.

Inside the shed, Persimmon is waiting at the edge of the pen, her little bushy tail wagging. Jules hurries to her and touches noses with her. Her long lashes flutter, and she lets out a happy bleat at seeing me with the bottle. Persimmon knows the drill now and is eager to eat.

As I sit by the fawn and give her the milk, with Jules by her side and Max looking on, I let out a huge sigh. Even though it's been stressful and tiring to take care of Persimmon, we've managed to keep her alive and happy for almost a week. Now I just have to keep doing this and everything will be fine.

CHAPTER THIRTEEN

The next morning, as I come to the kitchen to help with breakfast, Mom's and Dad's strained voices cut through the clatter of the dishes. Lately, it seems like they argue most of the time, and I hate when they do, because it's usually about money. When I hear them worrying about how they're going to pay their bills, I feel like we're tottering on a rickety bridge over a gaping chasm.

"We have to make bigger changes," Mom says. "We should think big, like renovating the barn to have a space to hold special events like weddings."

"I think it's better to keep doing what we're doing, and improve slow and steady," Dad says.

"But slow and steady won't get us the star," Mom says. "You saw those other places we visited. The one with an entire English-themed bar in their basement, or the other one with a demonstration farm. That's more than repainting the inn—they're providing an experience that other inns don't."

"We don't need to compare ourselves to others."

"You think this is just a fun hobby?" Mom says. "We need the star, otherwise we won't get the loan and our inn is in jeopardy."

"Let's get the basics down before we spend money to upgrade."

"We also need the money for basics like getting decent Internet access," Mom says.

I clear my throat. My parents stop arguing and turn to me, but I can still feel the tension between them.

"Good morning, Sienna," Mom says.

"Are we in trouble with the inn?" I ask.

"We're not, and there's nothing to worry about." Dad sets a bowl in front of me. "Cereal?"

I nod and grab the box of Crispix from the counter. The tension in their voices makes me not believe them. Now I *really* can't tell them about Persimmon. From what I just heard, we need more money to keep the inn in business. Mom and Dad have worked so hard to start up and make the bed-and-breakfast a success. If it fails, they might have to sell it. I don't want to end up without a home or my parents without a way to make money. They're distracted enough, and I don't want to add to their stress.

I'll keep my secret and focus on helping them as much as I can.

I pour the milk. "What can I do to help?"

"We just need to be prepared in case the accreditors come by," Mom says.

One couple left this morning, but two other couples plus Max and his mom are here this weekend, so I help my parents make breakfast. After we bring the dirty dishes to the kitchen island, Mom says, "Sienna, will you finish cleaning up from breakfast and change the sheets upstairs? Dad and I have an appointment with an architect for the barn renovation."

Dad rolls his eyes. "Not that I think we need to do this."

"Sure." As I clear the dishes, I frown. This constant sniping between Mom and Dad feels more serious than normal. What if they fight so much, they end up separated or divorced? Getting the seal will ease our money woes that are the root of all their disagreements. I take a deep breath.

I'm moving the dishes into the sink when Max

and his mom stop by to ask me to join them to visit her research site.

The curiosity and excitement I felt when Max and his mom talked about the forests last night comes rushing back. "I'd love to. Give me a minute." I take just enough time to finish piling the dishes into a tottering heap. I'll be back later to finish up.

Max's mom drives us twenty minutes away to a wooded area close to the regional park. As we get out, she explains, "We're doing a mushroom survey here. I'll show you where we rope off the sample areas called transects, and count the mushrooms we find inside."

As soon as I walk into the woods, the whisper of the leaves above and the crunch of dried ones underfoot calm me. A bird chirps and something rustles nearby. My worries about my parents melt away. I can see why people think forests are like natural cathedrals.

Max is filled with his usual nervous energy, skipping between the trees and chattering nonstop. He bounces on his feet. "No bug repellant today, huh?"

I was so busy this morning that it slipped my mind. "I guess it's not the end of the world if we don't use it."

"Whoa! Sienna Chen, are you chilling out?" Max laughs and does a weird jig. "You know, this confirms a theory I have that people *can* change, if they want."

"Do you always talk this much?" I ask, but with a smile in my voice.

"This? This is nothing. I can talk and talk without stopping. My record for talking nonstop without someone interrupting was four hours, on a drive to visit my grandparents, though that kind of drove my parents up a wall."

"I bet. You don't know me yet. How do you know if I've changed?"

Max gives me a considering look. "I don't know you too well, but I already *get* a lot about you."

I press my lips together. I'm not sure I like the idea of being so easy to figure out. "What do you think you know about me?"

"You like rules and order."

"Yeah, they make things predictable."

"And I like to go with the flow." He sweeps his arms around. "Be one with it all."

I give him a skeptical look. I worry that if I go with the flow, I'll be swept away.

Max pushes ahead and stops short. He grins and calls me over. "Check this out."

"What is it?"

"You'll see. Look." Max points. Bright orange mushrooms in multiple layers, like a giant pulpy rose, ring the base of the trunk of a tree. I've never seen them before.

"What kind of mushroom is that?"

"It's a *Laetiporus*."

"A what?"

"It's called chicken of the woods."

"Can you eat it?"

"Usually."

"What does that mean? Is it poisonous?"

"Should we find out?" He reaches for it like he's about to pick it.

"Ew, no. Max, why are you like this?"

"Like what?"

I laugh. "Like a weirdo who doesn't answer questions normally."

"Okay, some people are allergic to these mushrooms, and if you don't know much about mushrooms, it's not a good idea to eat them off the forest floor."

"Well, I knew that."

Max's mom points out a downed log and shows us some turkey tail mushrooms—gray, fan-shaped mushrooms with orange rings, stacked on top of one another. I've seen them before in the forest by the inn. "Here's an example of how important the fungi are," Dr. Klein says. "You can't see it, but they're breaking down the logs. Eventually, the log rots and becomes a habitat for insects and later, mulch for new growth." She pushes a soft spot on the log. "Here, feel this."

I come over and feel the squish beneath my fingers and imagine the filaments of the fungi spreading through the wood and working hard to break down the log. "It's spongy!"

"The fungi breaks down the lignin, which is the part of the wood that gives trees their firmness," Max's mom explains. "Want to hear something else cool? There are stages of forests, and the mycorrhizal networks play an important part in telling the trees when the soil is ready for the next stage."

"How do they do that?" I ask.

"The trees use the fungi connected to the roots of other trees to let them know about the soil conditions," she says, "and the trees that like specific conditions will grow into those areas."

"That's wild," I say. "It's like the trees are gossiping with each other about how good the soil is around them."

"Yeah!" Max deepens his voice and pretends to speak in Tree. "'Yo, my birch friends, check out this scrumptious soil. It's more delicious than a chocolate mousse cake.'"

"'Ooh, I'll head right over,'" I add in my Tree voice. "'I love a delicious dirt buffet.'"

We giggle.

Max's mom laughs. "And they've been doing this since the very first forests on Earth," she says.

It's amazing that these underground tendrils helped create this wonderful forest ecosystem. To think that all these webs under the forest floor connect trees together, and the only clue that all this is happening is the mushrooms that pop up in rotting logs or tree trunks.

When we get back, Max and I go to check on and feed Persimmon. I briefly think about the mess in the kitchen and the sheets I still need to change, but I'll get to that stuff later. Jules runs up to greet us and drops the items he's carrying.

I pick them up. "Look, Jules brought some more treasures here to show his friend."

"They're more pieces of pottery, like the ones he found before." Max turns to me. "There must be stashes of these around your land. Can we go look for more?"

I nod, but my annoyance flares at the memory of Max claiming the piece Jules had found before. I don't want to get into another fight about who owns the pieces again. "Yeah, maybe later. Let's take care of Persimmon first." I should probably get back to the inn to help my parents, but I'd rather spend the time with Jules and Persimmon. My parents won't miss me.

After I unlatch the gate to the puppy pen that holds Persimmon, instead of going to his friend like he usually does, Jules runs back out of the shed.

"What's up with that?" I say. "He usually can't wait to see Persimmon."

Max shrugs. "Don't know. He seems to be on a mission." His face lights up. "A Dog on a Quest! That's the name of my band, if I ever were to start one."

Before we can wonder more, Jules comes back to the shed with a mouthful of dandelion plants, complete with sunny yellow flowers.

"Jules, what are you doing?" I ask. "What's that?"

Jules looks up at me with twinkling eyes and trots to Persimmon's pen.

I let Jules in, and he drops the dandelions in front of Persimmon.

"He brought food to Persimmon!" Max shakes his head. "Jules is smarter than he looks."

I laugh in delight. "I've always known he's smart. This just shows he's also the kindest dog in the world. He wants to feed and take care of Persimmon!"

Persimmon walks over to the weeds, noses them experimentally, and begins to chew, her tail wagging while she eats.

Jules stands there, like a proud big brother.

I smile. The sight of Jules and Persimmon loving each other makes all the stress of taking care of the fawn worth it. It even blows away my worries about Mom and Dad fighting over the inn, because how can I keep my mind on those things when my sheepadoodle and an adorable fawn are such instinctive besties?

"Here, I'll feed her." Max holds out his hand for the bottle of milk.

I'm not sure why, but I don't want to give the bottle to him. But I don't have a good reason to refuse, so I hand it over. "Be careful with how you hold the bottle," I say. "Persimmon likes it when you hold it up high."

"I know," Max says. "I've figured it out."

I busy myself with changing the water pan and bringing some fresh hay to the pen.

"I still think Persimmon's ready to go out," Max says. "She's been trying to follow us out when we leave the shed."

I shake my head. "She's not ready yet. She's safer here." The thought of changing things up when everything's working makes my palms clammy. "Look how happy she is."

When Persimmon has had enough of the milk, Jules comes over with a rag. Persimmon bites on it, and the two begin a game of tug-of-war. Jules is much bigger and stronger, but he lets Persimmon think she has a chance. When he pulls the rag away from her, she bleats an indignant *weah*. He barks and immediately brings it back and urges her to go again. She takes him up on the offer and they pull back and forth at the rag, their tails wagging away.

"She's happy, but she could be even happier if we let her out," Max says.

I open my mouth to argue, but my phone rings—it's Mom. I stiffen. She usually texts me if she needs anything. Phone calls are serious.

CHAPTER FOURTEEN

"Sienna, we just got a call that the accreditors are on the way to the inn. We just got back ourselves." The tension from Mom's voice oozes through the phone.

"When will they be here?"

"In about fifteen minutes. Come back to the inn to help us get ready."

I leap to my feet. "Of course." I hang up and dash to the door. Jules chases after me and crashes into the side of the pen. "Jules, stay. I've got to go."

Jules stops at my command, but Persimmon follows Jules and stands near him, on her side of the pen. The pair stare at me with pleading eyes. "No, Persimmon, you can't come either. Please, stay quiet."

"I'll finish up here," Max says.

I press my lips together and nod. "Okay, thanks." I hurry back to the house, smoothing down my shirt and shorts. I don't know what I'm supposed to wear on a visit from hotel accreditors, but I'm a mess from sitting in the hay with Persimmon and Jules.

As I approach the house, Mom gives me a once-over and presses her lips together in disapproval. "We came back to this dirty kitchen."

"I'm sorry, I was with Max and his mom." I kick myself for not getting back to my chores before going to the fawn.

"What about making the beds?"

"Oh no. I forgot." Mom's disappointment chills me like a bucket of ice.

"The accreditors are going to be here any minute," Mom says. "Sienna, what is wrong with you? You're usually so organized and reliable, but first it was leaving the goat barn a mess, and now this."

Mom's words are like a punch and I want to explain everything, but I shake my head and swallow hard. I can't tell them that I've been spending all my time with a fawn. They won't understand. "I'm sorry, I can explain, but not now. I'll go up and make the bed."

Mom looks around the kitchen and shakes her head. "You do that. Dad and I'll clean up here." Again, I feel the sting of her disappointment. She and Dad bustle around the kitchen to tidy up, and Nainai straightens the books in the sitting room.

I take the stairs two at a time. Upstairs, I strip the bed in the room that's been recently vacated. I also pull out some towels to make some towel animals—I'll work on my simpler designs to get them ready in time.

It isn't long before the doorbell rings, and Mom and Dad greet the accreditors. I peer down the banister to catch a glimpse of them. They're a pair, a man and a woman. The man has dark brown hair and wears a light blue button-up shirt and tan pants; he looks like he's stepped out of a car insurance commercial. The woman is older, her stern expression matching her gray outfit of a blouse and pants and a thin strand of pearls. They look awfully formal compared to my parents, and definitely compared to me. Now I really wish I'd changed into something nicer.

"Hello, I'm Jaime Martinez, and this is my colleague, Stacy Hillsong." The man hands Dad his business card.

"Come in." Mom leads them to the sitting area and their voices drift into a murmur.

In my rush to take the bundle of soiled sheets and towels out of the room, I trip over a low table in the hallway by the banister.

I wince at the clatter as the table topples.

"What was that?" Ms. Hillsong says from below.

The accreditors and Mom and Dad look up from the bottom of the steps. "Is everything alright?" Dad asks.

"I'm fine." I toss the bundle of dirty items back toward the room, out of sight of the accreditors, and rub my shin where I'd run into the table. I wave. "I'm Sienna. Don't mind me." I set the table upright and fumble to rearrange the soaps that have fallen. I retreat, but not before seeing the man arch an eyebrow and write in his notebook.

"Why don't you come down, honey?" Mom says in a strained voice.

"In a moment," I call out as cheerfully as I can. I can't leave the room unfinished, and the accreditors might be up soon. I haven't made the bed up yet, and the pile of used sheets and towels lies by the door.

Out of the corner of my eye, a motion in the backyard catches my attention. I look out the window.

And gasp.

Jules is barking and running around, and Persimmon is out on the lawn, cavorting with him! The fawn must've had so much pent-up energy, because she and Jules run around each other in circles. They scamper around the yard, having the time of their lives.

I could've sworn that I latched the shed door when I left it, but it must've popped open. And somehow Persimmon must've come out of the pen inside. My mind immediately goes to Max. He must've let her out—he's been pushing for Persimmon to leave the shed, and he seems to do what he wants when it comes to the fawn. I rush out of the room. I have to go outside and get Persimmon out of sight before my parents or the accreditors see them.

I run down the stairs and rush through the living room where they are sitting to the patio door.

"Sienna," Mom says brightly. "Would you like to say hi to Mr. Martinez and Ms. Hillsong?"

"Hi, nice to meet you." I greet them to be polite, but I can't help looking out the window. Outside, Jules runs around in circles, barking playfully, and Persimmon follows on her spindly legs. Persimmon is clearly loving all the space and freedom as she runs around. Jules is as excited as I've ever seen him.

"Excuse me a moment." I open the sliding door to the backyard. I'm going to try to get Jules away from Persimmon and hope the accreditors don't notice.

Out on the deck, I whistle and call, "Jules, come back!"

Jules looks up and runs to me cheerfully. *Whew.* He's always such a good dog and listens to me.

As he runs over, my heart stops.

Persimmon runs after him!

Maybe she's confused being outside and wants to stick with him. Maybe she loves him so much that she follows him everywhere, as she's done the past two weeks every time she sees him in the shed. She runs after him and straight to me.

I back into the inn.

Jules barrels in.

The fawn seems to have tunnel vision, because she follows Jules right through the sliding doors and into the sitting room!

Mr. Martinez, Ms. Hillsong, and my parents freeze in utter shock.

Persimmon realizes that she's in a completely unfamiliar setting with a bunch of strange humans. She seems scared now and scampers erratically around the living room.

Jules whirls around the room and barks.

My parents jump to their feet. Ms. Hillsong backs away.

Mr. Martinez scrambles after the fawn. "There's a wild animal in the house. It's a fawn!"

Persimmon panics and crashes onto the coffee table and then the end table, knocking over the lamp. Her leg sweeps one of Mom's prized Wedgwood vases, which tumbles to the ground . . . and shatters into a thousand pieces.

Mom makes a horrified O with her mouth, and I wince.

Jules runs in and among the legs of the accreditors and jumps up on them, trying to keep them away from Persimmon. I chase after my dog.

"What is going on?" Dad yells.

"Jules, come here!" I shout.

"I'm so sorry, I don't know how this fawn got in here." Mom tries to corral Persimmon, but Jules gets in her way.

"This is ridiculous," Ms. Hillsong says.

In the chaos, Persimmon escapes to the kitchen. Jules follows her. The chairs clatter. The accreditors yell, and Mom and Dad try to calm them.

I run into the kitchen.

Persimmon hides under the kitchen table, and Jules stands guard.

I grab his collar. "Jules, we need to go out. Bring Persimmon with you. Come on." I push him to the kitchen door and hold it open.

He gets the idea and goes back to the table and scooches in between the chairs. He brings his nose close to Persimmon, who's stricken with fear. She's not moving. He licks her reassuringly and nudges her.

After a moment, she toddles to her feet and comes out from under the table.

"That's it," I say in a low voice. "Come, Jules."

Jules follows the sound of my voice, but he makes sure Persimmon follows him. Both of them leave the house by the side door. Mom, Dad, Mr. Martinez, and Ms. Hillsong appear at the kitchen door.

"Sienna, do you know anything about this?" Dad fights to keep his voice even-keeled, trying to keep calm in front of the visitors, but I can tell he is seething.

My insides roil like a mini thunderstorm. My palms turn clammy. "Um, I don't know how this fawn got in here. I'll go get Jules." I rush out of the kitchen, unable to face his ire, and let the door slam behind me.

Jules and Persimmon run down the hill, toward the forest.

Max comes running over, his expression halfway between concerned and curious.

"What happened?" he says.

"What did you do?" I yell. "Why did you let Persimmon out?"

"I didn't." Max joins me. "I don't know what happened. Just heard all of this fuss and came to see what's going on."

As Persimmon runs away, Jules follows.

"Jules! Persimmon!" I call.

But it's too late. They aren't listening, and they've reached the tall grass near the woods. Persimmon's little head disappears, and Jules's fluffy black-and-white head and tail bounce through the grass as they bound into the trees.

CHAPTER FIFTEEN

I run after Persimmon and Jules, my thoughts a swirling hurricane.

It's all my fault they ended up inside the inn. I had called Jules, and Persimmon just followed the only being she trusted. No surprise, she panicked once inside. And I can't blame Jules for just wanting to play with Persimmon; to them, the whole yard must've seemed like a paradise compared to the cramped pen in the shed.

"Hold up," Max says. "I'm coming with you!" He practically flies to my side.

I look over at him. I don't believe that he had nothing to do with Persimmon escaping the shed. "I don't need you. You've done enough."

Max stops, a hurt look on his face. Then, a determined one. "You can't tell me what to do. I care about Persimmon just as much as you."

Persimmon pops out the far end of the tall grass and reaches the tree line.

Jules follows the fawn.

Max continues to trail behind me.

I don't have time to argue with him. I chase after the two of them, and Max's footsteps slap the grass behind me.

When we get to the trees, the animals are nowhere to be seen.

"Where did they go?" Max says.

I stop to catch my breath. "I don't know."

"Let's go find them; we can't leave Persimmon out here by herself," Max says. "Isn't it dangerous for a little fawn?"

I frown. "Yes, but Jules is with her. She should be okay for a bit." Even as I say it, I can hear the doubt in my own voice. "Let's go back and talk to my parents." I need to explain myself and smooth things over with them. I don't even know what the inspectors think about all of this. I scan the woods and reluctantly head back to the inn.

When we get back, Mom and Dad stand on the patio with grim expressions. The accreditors have left. Max, seeing my parents' thunderous faces, slips away. I toss him an annoyed look. He was the one who probably let Persimmon out, but I get it. They're my parents, not his.

"What was that fawn doing here?" Mom demands.

"What in the heck is going on?" Dad says.

I gulp. "I have no idea how Jules found that fawn." I can't explain everything to my parents—how I found Persimmon and saved her life and took care of her. If they learn the truth, I'll get in trouble for hiding her and lying to them, and they'll never trust me again. I wanted to prove to them that I could take care of Persimmon before I told them about her, and now I've shown the opposite. I feel bad I have to keep lying to them, but I have to go find Persimmon.

"Whatever chances we had to get our Star Innkeepers seal has vanished." Mom splays out her fingers. "Poof! Gone."

Dad presses his lips into a tight line. "How could it have been so bold to come inside? Maybe it has rabies."

"She doesn't have rabies." Persimmon came inside only because she trusts Jules completely, but I can't tell him that.

Dad gives me a questioning look. "She?"

I shake my head like I said something silly, hoping he overlooks what I just said.

"Sienna, we left you with only a few things to take care of today. You're usually so on top of things." Mom frowns. "And now it's a disaster—the rooms and kitchen are a mess, and Jules is out of control."

My shoulders slump. We go inside to clean up. Dad stares at the mess in the sitting room, picks up a book on the floor, and slumps onto the couch. "We've worked so hard, and I'm sure the Star Innkeepers think we're sloppy and unprofessional innkeepers."

Mom picks up a broken piece of her prized vase with a pained expression. "These are irreplaceable."

I grimace. I can't even offer to pay for it, because it'd take a gazillion years before I could make enough money to afford it.

Mom looks up. "That's not the worst part," she says. "The accreditors went over some recent reviews we'd gotten. We've been so busy since we came back that we hadn't checked." Her lips become a thin line. "This is how we find out we had a fire in the kitchen and the fire department had to come."

The fire! It already feels like ages ago, with

"I'm not worried about Jules. He'll be back," Dad says. "He never wanders off for long. Go to your room and catch up on schoolwork."

I bite my lip at the unfairness of my punishment. But even worse, I think of Persimmon, alone and scared in the woods. Maybe Jules is with her, but maybe he isn't. Persimmon isn't used to being outside anymore, and she needs me.

But I can't let my parents down again. They're already at the limit of their patience with me, and I want to prove to them that I can take care of things. I should listen to them and go to my room. If Jules is with Persimmon, he'll take care of her.

I trudge down the stairs leading to my room, but halfway down, I pause. The coyote is still out in the woods, and Persimmon must be traumatized by what happened today.

I have to go find her, even if it means defying my parents again. I head to my room to make a plan.

CHAPTER SIXTEEN

It's evening, and I pace around my room, stuck.

I can't take it anymore, so I sneak out of my room, and peer around. My parents are still cleaning up the mess, having cancelled the social hour they usually hold with the guests. The guests love it; it's one of the things they always mention in their reviews. Now it's one more thing I ruined today. But I can't let it stop me from checking on Persimmon. It's chilly out, so I toss on a thin jersey and sneak out of the house as quietly as I can.

It's sunset and about to get dark, so I have to go quickly before anyone notices I'm gone. I can't grab a water bottle, because I don't want to go up to the kitchen and risk being seen by my parents.

As I pad down the hill, footsteps sound behind me.

It's Max. "Where are you going? Your parents told my mom you were grounded."

"Yes, but I have to find Persimmon," I say. "Get back inside. My parents might see you." I'm on the edge of the yard, near the garden and chicken coop, but Max is right out in the open space.

"I'm coming with you," Max says.

"I can do this myself. You already made things bad enough when you let Persimmon out."

"I told you. I had nothing to do with Persimmon escaping."

"*Someone* must've left the latch to the pen open."

"It could've been you," Max says. "Maybe the latch was loose and you weren't careful with it."

I glare at him. "You were the last one with them."

We're jogging down to the tree line. "Do you want my help or not?" Max says. "Two of us looking is better than one."

Max may be right, but I'm still annoyed at him. "Fine." I run ahead, crashing into the woods. Instead of taking the usual trail, we go in where we last saw Persimmon and Jules disappear into the trees.

The forest floor is covered with leaves and twigs, and fallen logs and branches dot the ground.

"Which way do you think Persimmon went?" Max says.

I squinch my brows together. Max actually seems concerned, so my anger leaches out a bit. I need to focus on finding Persimmon. "We saw her run that way." I point to an area of the woods.

We hike in and walk for a while. We look all around and see nothing, so we walk deeper into the forest. The easiest way to find Persimmon is to look for Jules, so I shout, "Jules, come on, boy! Jules!"

We wait.

Nothing.

"Jules!" Max adds to my shouts.

We call for my sheepadoodle, but he doesn't come. That's odd. Jules has such good hearing that he'd hear us if he was anywhere nearby. An uneasy feeling snakes through me. "Let's keep going," I say.

A rustling sound comes from our left. I stop. "Shh. What's that?"

Max stops by my side and we listen.

A chill runs through me. It's some kind of animal, and nearby.

"Maybe it's Persimmon," Max says. "Let's check it out."

"That's not a good idea," I say in a low voice. "What if it's the coyote that was after Persimmon?"

Max shakes his head. "The sound's not big

enough to be a coyote. It's more of a fawn-sized sound."

"What makes you the expert?"

He heads toward the rustling sound.

I follow slowly, not feeling good about this.

Rustle. Rustle. SQUAWK. SQUAWK.

All of a sudden, a flurry of movement bursts from the underbrush.

A wild bird rushes out at us—it's a huge turkey! It's about three feet tall, with its tail spread wide, like an angry, feathered kite.

Max pulls me to a nearby tree. "Get behind this."

"What? No!" I yell. "We need to run!" I grab him and pull him away.

We scramble past each other and crash through the woods, away from the bird. I look back frantically, and it's still chasing us.

My heart is in my throat. My mind's a blank, except for the need to get away. So much terror, being chased by an angry, wild animal. 0/10. Would not recommend.

SQUAWK. HONK. HONK.

This turkey won't stop. I'm running out of breath. I scoot behind a large tree, and Max comes crashing into me.

I pick up a large branch and step out from the tree, brandishing it. "Get away!"

Max gets the idea and he yells at it too. "YAAAH!"

The wild turkey finally lets up and turns away. It squawks its annoyance as it leaves.

I let out a huge sigh of relief. Then I turn to Max. "Why'd you run us straight into that dangerous animal? You riled it up."

"I was just trying to find Persimmon. Remember, the little fawn we're trying to save?"

"I remember alright." I glare at him.

"Why did you run like a wild creature with your hair on fire?" Max says. "*You* riled up that bird. Probably kicked in his predator instincts."

"Since when are turkeys predators?"

"Whatever. Focus on finding Persimmon."

I look around, and my stomach sinks. The air has chilled with the sun's departure, the shadows have deepened, and the trees loom above us ominously. I have no idea where we are, now that we ran away in a panic. "Do you know which way we came from?"

"No, isn't this your woods? Don't you know where we are?"

"Not after you ran us into a feral turkey."

"I'm sorry," Max says. "How was I supposed to know your woods have kid-eating turkeys?"

"Ugh! Stop treating everything like a joke!"

"Okay, what about your phone? We could use GPS."

"There's no signal in the woods." I pace worriedly. I can't believe we're lost. "Do you have your phone?"

"No, I didn't have time to grab it when I saw you sneaking out," Max says. "Let's keep looking for Persimmon and Jules."

I'm worried about Jules. What if something happened to him?

The drone of crickets and the trill of tree frogs are beginning to sound like the start of a horror movie.

I pull out my phone and turn on the flashlight. "We better use this. So we don't trip on roots and stuff."

"How's your battery?"

I glance down and my throat tightens. "It's at five percent. That's not a lot."

"It's enough," Max says hopefully. "Let's go in a straight line so we aren't going in circles." He points to what seems like a random direction. "Let's go that way."

"How would you know that's the way? It could take us farther away from the house."

"At some point, we'll run into your neighbors, right? How large is your property anyway?"

"It's four acres, but the woods are part of a regional park, so if we go in the wrong direction, we could be lost for days."

"Do you have any better ideas?" Max says.

I sit down on a log and rub my temples with my hands. "I think we should stay put. When I was young, my parents always said if I was ever lost, I should stay in one place until they found me."

"But they meant if you were lost in a mall or a store, right? Do your parents even know you're out here?"

My shoulders slump. I feel like crying but don't want to break down in front of Max. What if we end up in the woods all night? I like camping, but this is not being cozy in a sleeping bag or eating s'mores by a campfire. It's sitting on a log in the middle of dark, damp woods, wondering if a bear might decide to look for a midnight human snack. It's not having any water to drink.

We could be in real trouble.

"I'm going to climb that tree to see if we can figure out where we are." Max points to a tree that towers over the others. He shimmies his way up, hooking his arms against the lower hanging branches and pulling himself up. He's making his way up slowly but surely.

"Be careful."

"Don't worry, I got it. Just a bit higher and I'll be able to see through some of these trees." Max is above my head now, and looking at him turns my hands clammy and my stomach queasy. I've never been good with heights.

As I wait for him, frustration wells up. I'm not going to just sit here and let fate play with us. I'm going to do something too. Jules has got to be here somewhere. I stand up and yell at the top of my lungs, "Jules! Help us, Jules!"

Nothing.

Max looks down from his perch. "I'll join in."

"Okay, on the count of three. One, two, three." We yell as loudly as we can, "Jules! Jules! JULES!"

I strain to listen for Jules. The crickets and frogs

quieted when we started yelling, so all we hear is the rustling of leaves.

Then I hear it.

In the distance, a bark. The wonderful, amazing bark of Jules, growing louder as he comes closer.

"It's Jules!" I shout.

"Woo-hoo!" Max raises his arms up like he's won a prize.

A shape comes running through the woods—a fluffy, adorable sheepadoodle shape.

"Jules!" I yelp as Jules barrels into my arms. I bury my face into his neck and hug him, relief flooding through me. I didn't realize how scared I've been until I see Jules.

Then a thunderous crash.

Max lands next to me in a sickening heap. He's fallen out of the tree.

CHAPTER SEVENTEEN

My heart stutters. I rush to Max, who's landed on a bush.

"Are you okay?" My mind races with all the possible horrible outcomes: He's unconscious, he's broken his legs, he's in a coma . . . I kick myself mentally. If only I'd done something differently, he'd be safe. I should've set out ground rules for tonight, like no climbing trees or not coming along in the first place.

He's sprawled in the branches, limbs splayed out, and almost to the ground. "I think so?" Max's voice is unsteady as he pushes himself awkwardly out of the bush. Thank goodness he's talking and moving.

I hurry over to help him, but as soon as I touch his elbow, he winces. "My arm!" He falls back into the bush, clutching his left arm.

Jules circles us both excitedly and comes over to Max, licking his face.

I reach over and give him my shoulder and arm to help him stand. Max's face is strained with pain.

"I did something to my shoulder or arm," he says. "It hurts to move it."

"Can you walk?" I ask. "Are you alright otherwise?"

Max gets up gingerly, checks himself, and takes a few halting steps. "I'm okay." He looks up at the branch he fell from and his eyes go wide.

"Yeah," I say. "That was a long fall."

The dark presses in on us. I try to turn on my phone's flashlight, but the battery is dead. We're lost in the woods, we haven't found Persimmon, and now Max is hurt.

Jules whines and heads away from us; he wants us to follow him. It's dark, so he almost disappears in the shadows.

"Are you taking us home or to Persimmon?" I ask him.

Jules comes back and tugs at my shorts. He seems to be saying, *Follow me. I'll help you find what you need.*

"What do we do?" I say. "It seems like Jules wants to lead us out of here, but can you walk?"

"My legs still work," Max says. "Let's follow him." He gets going but stops, his face pale.

"Are you alright?"

"My shoulder and arm really hurt."

My mind races. I look around to see if there's anything I can use to help Max. Then it comes to me. I pull off my jersey. "I think I can make a sling out of this for you."

I know he must be in pain, because for once, he doesn't have a snappy joke.

"Here." I make a small hammock out of the jersey and tie the two sleeves together around his neck, carefully tucking in the extra material.

Max smiles wanly. "That feels better. How did you know how to do that?"

I shrug. Making a sling out of a shirt was filed in my memory, along with the videos about dealing with quicksand and shark attacks.

We follow Jules, going much more slowly than my sheepadoodle wants. Jules keeps darting ahead and then back to us.

After about ten minutes, Jules gives a bark that sounds like a yelp. It isn't his usual friendly bark. Something is wrong. Jules is whining and not happy. He circles around a downed log.

When we get there, we see what's upset him so.

My breath hitches. It's Persimmon, but she's stuck

in a dense mess of bushes. One of Persimmon's legs is caught in the crook of a branch, and she's starting to thrash.

"Shh," I say softly. "Please don't panic." I hold out my hand and try to move slowly to not further frighten the fawn.

Max slowly comes over. I can't believe both he and Persimmon are hurt.

The night closes in on us. I shiver, the hairs on my arm standing on end, even though the night air is warm.

"I'm going to try to untangle her leg." I crouch close to Persimmon and reach out to her.

She bleats, *weah! weah!* She lets me get close and touch her, but when I try to pull at the branches trapping her, she panics and struggles.

"I know your arm is hurt, but do you think you can help keep her still with your other arm?"

"I'll try." Max edges over and puts his right hand on Persimmon, who thrashes. Max groans and falls back, shaking his head. "Hurts."

I sit back. "I'm sorry I asked." Poor Persimmon— she's gone through so much in the last week, from losing her mother to being in a strange shed, and now trapped under the branches. I tried to do everything right by her, and look at where we are. My careful plans to keep her safe have backfired, and she's in worse trouble than she probably would've been if I hadn't meddled. And now Max is suffering too.

"You should go get help," Max says. "I'll stay here with Persimmon. I bet Jules can lead you back to the inn."

I stare at him and shake my head. "We can do this, Max. Let's not split up." I don't want to leave both Max and Persimmon behind. Once we leave, I may not find him again. Plus, I've kept Persimmon safe up until now, and all we need to do is get her back to the shed.

I approach Persimmon again and she thrashes.

Jules circles her and licks her face. This settles the little deer. Persimmon goes still.

"Thank you, Jules. You always know exactly what to do for Persimmon." I carefully pull the branches away from Persimmon until she's free. The fawn lets me help her because Jules is by her side. Persimmon tries to stand but her leg buckles.

"Something's wrong with her leg!" I say.

"What do we do now?" Max asks.

My thoughts race. Whether or not Max had a hand in Persimmon's escape, this is really all my fault. Why was I so stubborn about doing everything myself? If I'd told my parents about Persimmon or had tried harder to get ahold of the wildlife rehabilitator, they might've helped keep Persimmon safe. I'll never live with myself if something terrible happens to Persimmon.

I take a deep breath and try to push away my regrets. I can't leave Persimmon out here by herself with an injured leg. "Let's get her back to the shed." I gently pick her up.

Persimmon struggles briefly, but Jules licks her, which calms her down again. She seems to know that I'm trying to help, because she stops fighting me and lays her head on my chest. My breath catches—she trusts me!

I walk and stagger under her weight.

"I wish I could help," Max says.

"It's okay. Jules, take us home."

Jules understands and leads us through the darkness.

I carry Persimmon awkwardly back through the woods. It's slow going, because I don't want to trip, Max is hurt, and we don't have a light.

As our steps fall into a soothing rhythm, Persimmon's heartbeat calms down. Even though my arms feel like lead, my heart sings.

It doesn't take as long as I feared—maybe we *have* been going in circles—and we're back at the edge of the woods, right near the shed. Closer to the house, beams of flashlights cross one another and our parents are yelling, "Sienna! Max!"

It's a huge relief to see them. But I gulp. "Let's get Persimmon into the shed and then deal with your mom and my parents." I feel terrible ignoring them, worry lacing through their cries, but I can't deal with their questions now.

We make it to the shed, with Jules leading the way.

Max opens the door and we both awkwardly enter.

Max turns on the light, and I lay Persimmon down in her pen. My arms are rubbery. She immediately sits, as if she can't bear her own weight. Max sinks down onto a bag of goat feed, wincing in pain.

I grab a bottle of milk and offer it to Persimmon.

She turns her head and refuses it.

I stare at her. I'm in over my head now. Persimmon could be hurt. Plus, I still have to let my parents know we're alright. And we need to deal with Max's shoulder. "Let's get help for Persimmon." Persimmon had stood unsteadily in the woods after we'd freed her from the thicket, but now she doesn't seem to want to stand. I'm not a deer expert. There might be some other damage that I don't know about.

"No. We can take care of her by ourselves," Max says. "I don't think anything is wrong with her. She's just scared."

I stare at him. "Why don't you want us to get help?" My worries about Persimmon are mounting and I'm feeling overwhelmed.

Max looks uncomfortable, like he doesn't want to give me a straight answer. After a moment, he says, "You and I are a team, and we've been great together. If we get others involved, they'll take Persimmon away from us. It's our special thing." He looks at me pleadingly. "We can do this."

My heart does a little flip. I've never had a special thing with any of my old friends, and this really matters to him. Maybe Max is right. He *has* been more of a help than not, and we can take care of her again. Maybe it's best to keep our secret a little longer, at least until we're sure she's okay. I smile wryly. "We've been great, even after you fall out of a tree and hurt yourself?"

Max shifts and pain flashes across his face, but he returns my smile. "This? Ha ha, it's nothing. Who needs a left arm anyway? Way overrated."

I laugh despite everything.

He turns serious. "I'll show my mom my arm and she'll know what to do. For now, let's leave Jules here. He can keep Persimmon company while we deal with our parents. We can take care of her."

I stare. After a long moment, I let out a heavy breath. "Okay. We won't get my parents involved with Persimmon just yet. We've been doing a great job with her, so we can keep it up." I'm not sure I believe my own words, but I really want to, so I let Max convince me.

"That's what I'm talking about."

Max and I ease our way out of the shed and head up to the house with Jules following us. As we get halfway up the hill, Dad yells, "Sienna!"

We stop as the adults come from around the side of the house. Mom runs to me and gives me a fierce hug, and then yells at me. "Where were you? What were you thinking?"

Max's mother hurries over, her face pale with worry. She sees Max with the makeshift sling. "What happened?"

"I'm fine, Ma," he says. "I fell and hurt my arm."

"What's gotten into you? We were so worried." Dad grips me by my shoulder, whether out of relief or anger, I don't know. "Why were you two out so late at night?"

Max and I exchange glances. We haven't come up with a cover story, but we've agreed not to share Persimmon with them. "I'm sorry. Max and I wanted to look for Jules."

"And then I got hurt, which is why it took us awhile to get back," Max adds quickly.

I hope our parents don't think too much about our story, because the timeline probably doesn't add up.

"We'll take a look at your arm." Dad narrows his eyes at me. "There was a fawn. Was that what you were after? What was it doing here?"

"I don't know," I say. "Jules must've come across it in the woods. It ran away." I shrivel with each lie, but Mom and Dad are going to be livid if they learn I've been harboring Persimmon in their shed. That she's there now. They're already mad enough, and I can't stand the thought of them being even more angry and disappointed in me. Max and I will take care of Persimmon over the next few days, and when they've calmed down, we'll tell my parents about the fawn.

Jules runs around us eagerly and breaks away toward the shed.

"Jules, come here," I say sharply. Luckily, he's well-trained and always wants to please, so he comes loping back. I reach down and give him a huge hug.

As we walk back to the inn, Mom sighs. "We have to deal with the Star Innkeepers accreditors."

I gasp. In the chaos, I'd almost forgotten the surprise visit of the accreditors. "Did they send in their review already?" Even as I ask the question, I can tell from my parents' pinched faces what the answer is.

"No, but they made it clear we didn't get a star," Dad says.

"I'm so sorry!" I say. "It was all my fault. I messed up."

Mom shakes her head. "We don't blame you. We should've been around to prepare for the visit." Her brows furrow. "It was bad luck with the fawn coming along."

I gulp. Jules and Persimmon playing in the yard and crashing into the inn was definitely my fault, and it was probably what sealed our doom. "What does it mean that we don't get a star?"

"It'll be harder for us to get a loan that we were counting on to make improvements," Mom says. "We have to scale back on our plans."

"Will we lose the inn?" I knew it. We might lose our livelihood, and if so, I don't know where we'd live. I can't believe all of this might happen because of my selfishness, caring for Persimmon over my responsibilities to the bed-and-breakfast, to my family.

"We'll see," my dad says. "We'll figure out a way." While his words say one thing, his expression and tone say the opposite.

"Can we ask the accreditors to come back? Shouldn't we be able to get a second chance?"

Mom shakes her head. "It doesn't work that way. They come around once a year. We had our chance."

"That's so unfair," I protest. I've blown it. Worse, there's still Persimmon to worry about.

Max's mom fusses over him, hovering with alarm and worry. "Why did you run off like that?" She gives me side-eye, like I'm to blame.

I want to protest at the unfairness of her assumptions. Max was the one who followed me.

Jules runs over to me and snuggles into my side. I bury my face in his fur and hug him gratefully; he can always tell when I need a boost.

"I'm so sorry this has happened," Dad says. "I can drive you two to urgent care to see about his arm."

Dr. Klein shakes her head. "It's fine, I'll take him." As she and Max walk to their room, he turns to me and gives me a small wave with his good hand.

Mom and Dad spend the rest of the night talking in low, tense voices. They keep me under their watch, so I can't sneak out to the shed to make sure Persimmon's okay. Poor little fawn—how stressful it must have been to be in the woods after being protected in her shed for the past week, and then injuring herself.

I go to bed filled with unease and worry for Persimmon.

CHAPTER EIGHTEEN

I spend a restless night tossing and turning. I wonder how Max is doing. Their car pulled in after I went to bed, so it was too late to check on him. Whenever I hear a noise outside my window, whether it's cicadas or an owl's hoot, I wonder about poor Persimmon. Even though Persimmon is safe inside her shed, I imagine the fawn is also listening to these strange noises and is spooked. If Persimmon is hurt or in pain, she could be in danger.

I finally drift off to sleep.

When I wake, Persimmon is the first thing on my mind. Mom and Dad insisted last night that they'd do the morning farm and breakfast chores—probably since they can't trust me anymore. I'd normally appreciate that, but now I don't have an excuse to go out to secretly feed Persimmon. I suppose what I've done is much worse than what I've ever done before so my parents are stumped as to how to give me consequences.

As I get dressed, I think about my predicament.

I can't go to school without checking on Persimmon, and I can't leave the fawn for the whole day. I need to know that she's okay. But I'm already in such trouble with Mom and Dad. If I sneak down to see her, I'll have to wait until after my parents are out of the way, which will make me miss the school bus. My small boulder of disobedience will turn into a landslide.

I pace around my room, flop on my bed, and scream into my pillow.

I sit up. I've made a decision—I'll skip school. I know this is another step in defying Mom and Dad, but Persimmon is more important than one of the last days of the school year. If I just get her over this hump, then everything will be fine.

After breakfast, I grab a bottle of goat milk from the storage room fridge and put it in my bag. I walk to the end of our long driveway to the bus stop as usual, but before the bus arrives, I walk down the road and back into the woods. I slip back to the house from the trees and head to Max's doorstep.

As I cross the lawn to the entrance to Max's addition, Jules comes bounding up.

I give him a hug and accept his kisses, while

glancing frantically at the house. "Hello, Jules."

Jules starts to run to the shed, but I call, "No, Jules. Come!"

He looks at me quizzically and comes back, wondering why I'm changing our routine.

I'm completely exposed. If Mom or Dad happen to look out the window of the front of the house, they'll see me and Jules at Max's porch. I knock urgently.

Max peers out the window, and his face lights up when he sees Jules and me.

"Please, let me in," I say. "I can't be seen."

Max steps aside, a delighted expression on his face. "Ooh! Are you in hiding? On the lam? Running from the law?" He's wearing a more professional sling than a jersey on his arm now.

"How's your arm?" I step into the sitting room part of their suite. "Is your mom around?" Jules investigates Max's shoes piled up by the door, and I pull him back.

"It's just a strain, so that's good. I didn't break anything." Max draws the shades. "Don't worry, I've seen a lot of shows; I know how to keep you hidden. My mom went to work early today, because she's coming back for lunch to check on me." He pets and ruffles Jules's fur with his free hand. "Hello, doggy. Running from the law too? I've got your back."

I snort. "It's not that serious. I just don't want my parents to see that I didn't get on the bus."

Max's eyebrows shoot up. "Ditching school *is* serious. Even I, a person who flouts convention and rules, don't skip school."

"It's important though. We need to make sure Persimmon is okay after her ordeal last night."

Max gets it immediately. "Right, I'll come with you."

I pace back and forth and peer around the shades. "Can we go in a bit? I want to wait until my parents go on their errands."

Max eases himself down onto the couch and props his feet on the coffee table. Jules jumps up and snuggles next to him. "Watch the arm, buddy. So, while we're waiting, what's the wildest thing you've ever done?"

"This, probably. I've never skipped school before."

Max grins. "Ooh, living on the edge! I love it."

I groan inwardly. I actually hate it. The day is off-kilter, not following its usual predictability. And it's all because of Persimmon. Ever since she came, my life's been a state of anxious worry and upheaval.

After what seems like an interminable time, Mom and Dad get into their car and leave down the driveway. I heave a sigh of relief.

"Okay, we can go now."

"What about your grandmother?"

"She'll be busy in the house. We can sneak down to the shed."

Max's eyes gleam. "We'll be like spies."

We step out, followed by Jules. When we reach the shed, the fawn's eyes are open and alert, and her ears turn in our direction. I'm so relieved that she's awake.

She bleats softly. If a fawn could smile, Persimmon does. She and Jules exchange happy greeting licks.

I kneel down. "Don't you just love her?"

Max reaches his hand out to pet Persimmon, and she gives his fingers a lick. "Yeah, she's cute. See? She's fine. We can take care of her by ourselves."

I'm still not sure. I bring out the bottle of goat milk and offer it to Persimmon.

The fawn turns her head.

This is unusual; it's not like Persimmon to refuse

the bottle since she's gotten the hang of drinking from it. Worry worms through me.

"Max, let's see if Persimmon can stand up."

Max comes over. "Let's have Jules leave her side. She always follows him."

"Great idea! Jules, come here." I open the pen to let him out. As he reluctantly follows me, Persimmon stays seated.

Jules returns to Persimmon and nuzzles at her.

Persimmon puts down her head, as if she's tired.

Worry and fear ooze through me. I've loved taking care of Persimmon and seeing her blossom over the last week, and I can imagine how wonderful it'd be to have her as a pet and a constant companion to Jules. Persimmon is so sweet and fun, and Jules has never seemed happier. And it even seems like the fawn likes me too.

But now something is wrong. Persimmon seems off, even sick. Last night probably traumatized her.

I look out the window of the shed, as if I can find an answer. My eyes wander to the goats out in the paddock. At the sight of Cocoa and Agatha, the memory of Persimmon drinking their milk pops up. And the delight and love between Jules and Persimmon when they played together.

Slowly, the pieces are coming together. The goats have helped Persimmon by giving her precious food. Jules has been her best friend and helped her from the beginning. He's the one who saved her from the coyote attack, calmed her enough for her to trust us to feed her, kept her happy in the shed even when she wanted to be outside, and found her when she fled to the forest.

Different animals helping one another is just like different trees helping one another through the fungi living in their roots to grow taller and stronger.

It hits me. The web of life is stronger and more interconnected than one single person or animal. It's the community that helps everyone thrive.

I've been trying to do everything by myself, and I don't have to do it all alone.

I've accepted Max's help, and that came with his own ideas and disagreements. Now it's time to accept even more help. I know what I have to do. I need to help the fawn—and fast.

Looking at Persimmon, I know deep down that

the right thing to do is to ask for help from a professional. It's time to face the consequences of having lied to Mom, Dad, and Nainai for all this time.

"We should go to a wildlife rehabilitator," I say. "Persimmon isn't drinking or standing and she may be hurt."

Max shakes his head. "Look, she's fine. She had a stressful time last night in the woods, but now she's back and safe. We took care of her before and we can keep doing it."

"But that's just it. She's not accepting our help," I say. "I don't want to wait until it's too late." I glare at Max. "Don't you even care about her?"

Max's expression darkens. "Just because I wasn't the one who found her doesn't mean I don't care. I care about her as much as you do."

"You don't act like you do." I can't believe how casual Max is being.

"Stop judging me because I don't do everything the way you want me to," Max says with heat in his voice. "And I didn't let Persimmon out yesterday. I swear. Do you trust me or not?"

That stops me cold. I don't know why every time

Max says something, my first instinct is to argue back. I think about everything he's done for Persimmon. How he's silly with her and feeds her while I'm at school. How he never does it the way I want him to, but Persimmon's as comfortable with him as she is with me. He has a touch with her and she trusts him. How he didn't hesitate to come into the woods with me to look for Persimmon, and how he's become a rock I've come to depend on.

There's no good reason for me to reject his arguments at every turn. He's the first person I've really connected with since we moved here, and he's going to be here for the rest of the month. I don't want to make the same mistakes I made with my old friends in D.C., where I always had to have the last word. I don't want to lose this new friendship we have. He makes me laugh and, together, we've managed to keep Persimmon safe up to now.

"I do trust you," I say.

But now I'm confused. I hate the idea of giving up and asking for help. Like maybe that'll prove I'm not good enough on my own. And Max has shown that he's a dependable friend. If I turn on him and ignore his opinion, I'll risk losing my only true friend.

But even though I've tried my best and researched how to take care of Persimmon, and even with Max's help, she still ended up getting hurt in the woods. She shouldn't have to suffer because we *hope* we can keep her safe.

Jules and Persimmon sit next to each other. Jules stands up and barks softly, trying to get Persimmon to get up and play with him. She turns away and lays her head down. It seems like she's exhausted.

My heart is caught in my throat. It's amazing that Max and I managed up to now, but Persimmon isn't eating, and I'm worried about her. I hate that I have to go against Max, but seeing her like this makes up my mind. I need some expert help.

The wildlife rehabilitator hasn't answered my calls, but maybe there's another adult who can help. Not my parents, because I'd have too much to explain. Max's mom, on the other hand, is kindhearted and is both a scientist and resourceful. She'll have good advice or can help reach the rehabilitator.

I glance at Max, who's crouched by Persimmon.

He's trying to get her to drink some milk, but the fawn is having none of it.

"You said your mom's coming back at lunchtime?"

Max gives me a funny look. "Why do you want to know?"

"Just curious," I say. "I have some questions for her."

He shrugs. "Yeah, she should be back soon."

I slump down. I've skipped school to take care of Persimmon, and now I have to wait hours for help.

"I'm going out," I say.

"Where are you going?" Max asks.

"For a walk. I need to figure things out."

"I'll stay here with Persimmon and Jules."

I feel a surge of resentment and confusion. I know he cares about Persimmon, but it seems like all he's doing is watching her suffer. I have to do more than that. I stalk out of the shed, unsure of where I'm heading, but anything is better than sitting around doing nothing.

CHAPTER NINETEEN

I head toward the house, but my steps slow. Nainai's at the inn, so I can't stomp back to my room when I'm supposed to be in school. I don't want to go back to the shed and get into an argument with Max again.

I stop by the paddock to see the goats, making sure I'm out of sight from Nainai's view if she happens to look out the window. The goats tend to hang out outside during the day and go back to the barn in the evenings, but when they see me, they gather and bleat, eager for food.

"You've already been fed today." I duck into the barn, out of view from the inn. The goats follow me. "Oh, alright, y'all are too much." I gather some alfalfa hay and put it in the feeding bin, and the goats set to chomping.

I sit down on a crate and pull out my phone. I try the rehabilitator again. I listen to the message: "Hi, you've reached Maite Santoja. If you have a small animal or bird, you can drop it off in the cages on the covered back porch. If you've found a larger animal, please leave a message at the tone, and I'll get back to you as soon as I can." The message ends with an address and a *beep.*

I'm so surprised that I didn't get the "out of town" recording that I hang up. My heart patters. I wasn't expecting to get through, so I wasn't prepared to leave a message. The fact that the messages have been cleared out, and I can leave messages, means the rehabilitator must be back in town.

Butterscotch stops what she's doing and comes over to me and bumps my knee. I scratch the goat's neck. "So glad you look better, Butterscotch." What a relief that Butterscotch is back to her normal self, eating and wanting attention. Mom must've called the vet and had the goat seen. At least that's one thing I don't have to worry about.

I get up and pace back and forth. I don't want to wait until Max's mom comes home for lunch, since that would be at least a couple of hours.

Then it comes to me—I'll call Max's mom and ask her for immediate help.

I run back to the inn and sneak into the house

from the back, where there aren't tinkling bells to notify Nainai of my entrance. I listen carefully to see if I can figure out where my grandma is. The main spaces are quiet, so Nainai is either upstairs or napping. I pad to the study, find the guest register, and look up Dr. Klein's number and put it in my phone.

I hurry back to the goat barn, glancing at the shed where Max still is, and ignore the brief urge to involve him. I know what he'd think about me calling his mom.

After a moment, I make the call.

"Hello?" Max's mom's voice is puzzled.

"Hi, Dr. Klein, this is Sienna Chen, from the inn."

"Is Max alright? Is it his arm?" Max's mom's voice is suddenly alarmed. "Why aren't you in school?"

"Everything's okay, don't worry." I gulp. "I'm sorry to bother you at work, but I didn't know who else to call."

"What's wrong? How can I help?"

I don't even know where to start. I take a deep breath and explain about the fawn—how Jules found Persimmon and how Max and I've been taking care of it. A pang goes through me when I think of Max. It takes a long time to explain, but finally it's done—and

I feel a whole lot lighter. "And now the wildlife reha-bilitator seems to be back, but she isn't answering her phone, and I was wondering if you could give me a ride out to see her."

After a long pause, Dr. Klein says, "I wish Max and you had confided in me earlier. We should talk to your parents and sort everything out."

"Please, I don't want to involve my parents yet. They have so much going on, with the accreditors and running their inn."

Another long pause. I scuff the hay at my feet and sink my head into my hands.

"Alright. I'm going to finish this transect and I can be back in about half an hour. I'll take you to see the rehabilitator."

"Thank you so much!"

"Max can join us too."

I swallow. Max and I have just fought, but I can't say no to his mom inviting him along. "Yeah, sure."

I hang up and heave a sigh of relief. Already, it feels like a burden is lifting. Dr. Klein has agreed to help, but now I have to face Max again. But I know that it was the right thing to do.

I go to the shed to tell Max about my call. He's got his arms around Persimmon and is trying to get her to drink from the bottle. My anger at him softens; his heart is in the right place. Even though it isn't doing any good, because the fawn is still not drinking.

I tell him about calling his mother and that we're going to see the rehabilitator.

Max glowers. "You're a traitor," he says. "Why did you go behind my back and tell my mother, of all people, about the fawn?"

"I thought she could help."

"You don't care about what I feel or want, do you?" Max says. "You could've included me."

I shrink back. "I'm sorry." All of my thoughts from earlier rush back. I feel terrible for not fully trusting Max, but my worry over Persimmon was stronger. "Persimmon needs more help than we can give her."

"You don't know that. I was about to get her to drink milk," Max says. "Plus, she's gotten used to us. She's not good with strangers."

Now my anger rises again. "You're not the one who found her. You're lucky I let you help me." Max helping with Persimmon has only complicated everything.

Max's eyes widen with hurt.

Immediately, I feel bad about lashing out at him, but I bite my lip. We don't speak until his mother comes back. I clamber into the back seat of her car. I don't regret calling her, because Persimmon needs this. I try one more time to make him see my point of view. "We need an expert's help, Max."

Max looks out the window, ignoring me.

Just as we're about to leave, Max says, "You know what, forget it." He unbuckles his seatbelt and opens the door. "You can go to your rehabilitator. You obviously don't need me."

"Honey," his mom says. But he's already out of the car and has shut the door. Dr. Klein turns to me. "Is everything okay with you two?"

I sigh. "I don't know. I'll talk to him later to sort it out."

She glances at her son, who's heading back to their suite. She nods. "I'm sure you two will work it out. Why don't you come to the front seat, and I'll take you to the rehabilitator."

I nod gratefully. We drive out to the rehabilitator's in silence, as Max's angry words echo in my head.

What I said to him was unfair, and I'll apologize to him when we get back. Soon, we reach a long, unpaved driveway near a wooded area, which leads to a house nestled among the trees. Parked in front of the car is a yellow Jeep with a license plate that says SAVWDLF. I try to distract myself by puzzling out what it stands for.

As we step out of the car and head up the path to the front door, it comes to me—Save Wildlife. This makes me feel better: This is someone who's dedicated herself to helping wild animals. When we get to the front, a sign on the door states, *Leave your small animal rescues on the back porch and sign into the log with your contact information*. A dog barks from inside the house, a sign that someone is home.

Dr. Klein rings the doorbell.

We stand awkwardly at the front step, until footsteps come to the door. A frazzled-looking woman in a messy ponytail, T-shirt, and shorts opens the door. "Yes?" She's slightly breathless, as if she has run to the door. "If you have a bird or small animal, go around the back and I'll meet you."

"We're here to ask about an abandoned fawn," I

blurt. I can't believe I'm speaking up like this to a stranger, but it's important. Persimmon's life is on the line.

An irritated look crosses the woman's face, but she smooths it out. "You should've called if you've found an abandoned fawn."

"I've been trying, but your voicemail has been full."

A distracted look flits across her face. "I'm sorry. My life is in shambles, between visiting my mom in the hospital and dealing with some shenanigans at my kid's summer camp . . . but I'm sure you don't want to hear the details. Anyway, I'm back and I've cleared the messages." The woman talks as if she doesn't stop to take a breath. "I'm Maite. What's your name?"

"I'm Sienna Chen."

"Tell me about this fawn."

I explain how Jules and I found the abandoned fawn a week ago and how Max and I've been taking care of her.

The woman frowns. "You know, fawns are usually not really abandoned by their parents when you find them alone."

"I know," I say, "but she was crying for milk and about to get pounced on by a coyote." I explain how we saved Persimmon and took care of her with goat milk and, even though it worries me that I'll seem incompetent, how Persimmon got free and ran into the woods and hurt herself.

Maite's face is serious as she listens. "How does the fawn look now?"

"She didn't drink milk today and seems listless, so I wanted to get your help."

Maite nods. "You were right to come to me before it's too late. It's not a good idea to take care of a wild fawn on your own. In fact, it's illegal to take in a fawn for more than twenty-four hours in the state of Virginia."

I feel myself wobble. I didn't know this. What if this woman calls the cops and has me arrested? "I'm sorry. I didn't mean to be a criminal."

Maite smiles. "We have the law for a reason, but I'm not going to get you in trouble. The important thing is you're here now."

Relief washes over me.

"While you're here, let me show you the fawns we

have." Maite walks briskly around the side of her house as we hurry to keep up with her. The back opens to a couple of large fenced areas around land that includes trees and branches and a shed. Inside one are about seven fawns that look bigger than Persimmon. Some nibble on grass and leaves from downed branches. A couple of others drink milk from bottles in a rack. "Let's stay back though," she says. "My goal is to get these fawns ready to go back to the wild by the end of the summer, so the less human contact they have, the better."

"Why is that?"

"When fawns get too used to people, they no longer fear them, and that's dangerous for when they go back to the wild," Maite says. "Or they become too attached and dependent on humans, so they hang around human neighborhoods, which is also danger-ous. They can get run over, shot, or otherwise hurt."

Now I feel even worse, mentally ticking off all the things I've done wrong. First, I broke the law by taking in Persimmon. Second, I gave her plenty of human contact by feeding her by hand and hanging out when Jules played with her. "I'm so sorry. I didn't know. I was just trying to take care of Persimmon."

She gives me a stern look. "You're very lucky, young lady, that you didn't kill this fawn."

I suck in a breath. "What?"

"Deer are prey animals, and their bodies will shut down with stress. So many young abandoned fawns die, not from injuries or other noticeable reasons, but from shock and human handling."

The blood drains from my face. I could've killed Persimmon! The thought is utterly chilling. "I'm sorry. I had no idea."

"Most people don't." Maite shakes her head and purses her lips. "Once, a young fawn was brought in that had been handed around a child's birthday party." Her expression darkens. "It didn't make it."

I gasp and tears spring to my eyes.

Maite's expression softens. "You were lucky, because fawns have different personalities and con-stitutions, and this one sounds like a hardy little thing. You also did some things right. You fed her goat milk, which is the best substitute for a mother deer's milk, and you kept her safe."

I blink rapidly. "I tried to call you, but—yeah,

thanks." My words tumble out in a hodgepodge, half apology and half explanation.

"There's a reason for the rules, Sienna," the rehabber explains. "There are so many cases where people think a fawn is abandoned when it really isn't. They do more harm than good by taking them in. Also, wild animals need to stay wild."

"She and my son did their best," Max's mom says.

Gratitude surges through me at her sticking up for me.

Maite looks at me kindly. "Now you know. How about you take me to see your fawn, and we'll know what we need to do. Even though I'm very full here, the best thing will be to take her in. Being around other fawns will help her stay wild and she'll have a family to be with when they're released at the end of the summer."

I gulp. I hate that I put Persimmon in danger, even though I was doing my best and had good intentions. It sounds like the right thing to do is to give up Persimmon so Maite can take care of her properly and keep her with her fellow fawns.

But the thought of losing Persimmon wrenches at

my heart. If Maite can check on her and see that she's okay, I don't see why we can't keep her. I bet Persimmon is so used to us humans that sending her back into the wild would be a shock to her system. Plus, I love Persimmon, and so does Jules. They bond more and more each day—Persimmon is so happy with her best friend and Jules is so proud to protect her. It's not often someone finds the friend of their soul. It doesn't seem fair to give the fawn up and break up such a special connection.

CHAPTER TWENTY

Maite drives back to the inn, following our car. As we park, Nainai comes out of the inn and stands at the front porch, a puzzled expression on her face.

Jules bounds out and greets us by running up to each person and leaning in for a big doggy hug. Even Maite gets his exuberant hello.

"Hello, there. Are you a good boy? I bet you're a good boy," Maite says as she ruffles his fur vigorously. I grin at how much she loves animals.

"Sienna? What are you doing home this early?" Nainai looks at Maite. "May I help you? Are you with the school? Is everything okay?"

Maite turns to me. "What's going on here?"

I gulp. "This is my grandmother, Joanne Chen. Nainai, this is a wildlife rehabilitator. She's here to help us with the fawn."

"The fawn?" Slowly, something dawns on Nainai's face, as bits of the puzzle must've come together. "You mean the one we saw Jules with when the accreditors were here? Is it here on our property?"

"Yes, Max and I've been taking care of her in the goat shed. I'll explain everything, but we need to hurry. This way." I head to the side of the house to go around to the back. Jules follows eagerly.

Max's mother drops back. "I'll catch your grandmother up on what's been going on and check in with Max. Meet you in a bit." She walks to the porch and speaks to Nainai in low tones.

I should go talk to Max as well, but I want to be there when Maite meets Persimmon.

Jules runs ahead, ready to play with Persimmon.

As Maite and I approach the shed, I feel shaky. Having Maite come and take charge should've made me relieved that someone who knows what she's doing can help Persimmon. But it just means that I'll be judged for my failure to keep the fawn safe. I felt bad enough learning all the things that could've gone wrong with Persimmon, and now it'll be confirmed that I'm a destroyer of fawns.

Maite Santoja walks into the shed and looks around at the setup. She goes into the pen, feels the fawn's body with experienced hands, looks at her eyes and ears, and gently pulls Persimmon to a standing position. One of Persimmon's front legs buckles, but she steadies herself. Maite says a few things under her breath.

"When was the last time she drank milk?"

I think back. Persimmon hasn't drunk from the bottle since before she got lost in the woods. "It's been over a day. She also hasn't moved from that corner." I shrink at what will surely be Maite's disapproval.

Maite gently pinches the scruff of Persimmon's neck. "She's not dehydrated, and she seems well-fed, yet you say she's refused the bottle." Maite looks around. "I see there's a pan of water. She must've gotten to it, but that wouldn't be enough nutrition."

The door to the shed flaps open, and Jules comes in, holding a mouthful of dandelion weeds and clover in his mouth. He nudges the latch of the pen and the door swings open. He goes into the pen and drops the greens next to Persimmon. Persimmon and Jules touch noses, and Persimmon chomps down on the weeds.

I let out a surprised laugh. "It's Jules! He's been feeding Persimmon." I slap my forehead. "And he was the one who let Persimmon out of her pen." I've really done Max wrong by blaming him.

Maite kneels down and gives Jules some hearty pats on his head and back. "You're some dog. Maybe I should hire you as a deer rehabilitator. Are you a good rehabber? Yes, you are." She turns to me. "Let's try the bottle again. Do you have one?"

"Yes, I'll get a fresh bottle." I run back to the inn.

As I warm it under the sink, Nainai comes by. "Oof, Sienna. You hid a lot from your parents and me."

I set down the bottle and my eyes threaten to water. "I'm so sorry, Nainai." Of all my family members, I feel like I've deceived my grandma the most. She's the one I straight up lied to the most while I snuck around to keep Persimmon hidden. "I wanted to do everything myself. I guess it made me think I had things under control."

Nainai's stern expression melts. "You don't need to say sorry to me. I should've figured out something was going on. And now you know sometimes you can ask for help."

I bury myself in her arms and a huge weight lifts.

"Also, it's your parents you should apologize to."

I swallow. The thought of facing my parents makes me queasy.

"Are you going to show me this fawn of yours?" Nainai says.

"Of course. Are you okay with walking down to the shed?"

Nainai pauses a moment, then nods to Max's mom. "Yes, I'll take my time and walk down with Susan. You go on ahead."

I give my grandmother another grateful hug and hurry back to the shed with the bottle of milk.

Back at the shed, Maite stands Persimmon up and holds the bottle above her head. "This is the best position to feed a fawn," she explains, "because it mimics the way a fawn feeds from its mother." Max and I have figured this out already, but it's good to hear the reason.

Maybe it's Maite's confidence or her soothing presence, but Persimmon reaches up and takes a sip, and then another, and before long, is gulping down her milk. Maite's eyes crinkle with pleasure. "I estimate this fawn is almost a month old, and it's time to have her grazing outside, instead of being stuck in this shed. I'll squeeze her into my place."

A pang shoots through me. I don't want to give Persimmon up. Not now, when she's doing great and both Jules and I have fallen in love with the fawn. An idea flashes through my mind. "Can I keep her here and take care of her, if my parents are okay with it? We can build her a fenced area." Dad is always puttering around and moving the goats around the property by building temporary enclosures, so I'm sure it won't be a problem. He probably won't mind, even if he says he hates deer. I hope.

Maite tilts her head and considers my request. "The fawn should really be with others. It's better for her to be with other fawns and learn how to be a wild deer. Our goal is to release her at the end of the summer when she's strong and able to fend for herself. She'll be living with a deer family, not a human one, so the sooner she gets used to other deer the better."

I'm stricken. The thought of having to give up Persimmon hits me in the gut.

"But I can see that your dog and this fawn have bonded," Maite continues, "and all in all, you've done well in taking care of her." Her brows furrow. "I am very full at the rescue and while it's possible, it will be tight to add this one to my group."

My heart lifts with each word.

Jules nudges his head into Maite's hand.

She turns to him, scritches at his neck, and laughs. "You sneaky boy. Trying to get on my good side to help your mama's case." Maite looks at me. "Okay, we can give it a go. But I'm going to need your parents to agree and follow my instructions on how to make a proper enclosure. They'll have to train as my apprentices for this to be legit."

I whoop. Jules's ears perk up and he gives me kisses.

"You'll have to change some things up," Maite says. "Fawns imprint on people very easily, and they'll forget they're wild. You'll have to create a setup that minimizes human contact."

I gulp. I love how Persimmon has lost her fear of me, and seeing Jules and the fawn play together is the highlight of my day. But I nod. "Yes, I'll do it." I'll do anything to keep Persimmon, even if the fawn doesn't turn out to be the pet I've hoped for. A little part of me wonders if maybe Persimmon will be able to keep playing with Jules anyway.

"I'll need to talk with your parents. When do they get back?"

"Any minute now." I sigh. I've put my parents out of my mind, but I have to face them and tell them everything. I'm already in deep trouble from disappearing into the woods last night, and now I've skipped school to get help for Persimmon.

"I'll hang out here with this little one and check her out more," Maite says. "Let me know when your parents return."

"Sure." I turn to go. "Come on, Jules."

My sheepadoodle looks at me and wags his tail, but stays put, his smile letting me know he's happy to stay with Persimmon.

Maite lets out a small laugh. "He can stay and help. Clearly, he knows how to take care of this little one. You're a good boy, aren't you?"

I grin. At the rate Jules is charming Maite, I'm going to have to worry about her wanting to adopt him. "I'll be back." I leave the shed, but instead of going into the house to wait for my parents, I go around the side to the suite. I have to talk with Max and apologize to him. Then I'll face my parents.

Untangling the layers of lies and hiding is not going to be fun.

CHAPTER TWENTY-ONE

At Max's porch, I knock on the door.

I stand there for what seems like an eternity until, finally, the door opens. Max stands there, not saying anything and making no move to let me in.

I clear my throat and take a deep breath. "I'm sorry I went around you, Max," I say. "I was desperate to help Persimmon, and you didn't want to get outside help."

Max frowns and looks away.

I expect him to be angry—to yell at me, even—but his silence is even worse. He's usually so exuberant and to see him shut down like this is chilling. I don't know what to say. But I need to reach him, because he's a true friend who didn't deserve the way I failed to trust him.

I realize that my weak apology was me blaming him, so I try again. "I'm sorry I didn't confide in you. I know you care about Persimmon so much, and she means a lot to you, and you were also trying to do what was best for her." I breathe out a heavy sigh. "And I should've believed you when you denied letting Persimmon out."

Max comes out and sits on the wicker chair on the porch, and I join him at the one next to it. He stares across the front lawn for a moment before he finally speaks. "You were right. I thought we could do it by ourselves, and I was being selfish too. Persimmon's life is more important than what I think." He looks over at me. "I just wish you'd trusted me to talk about going to my mom. I mean, it's *my* mom!"

"I guess I'm so used to trying to do things on my own, even after you started helping."

Max gives me a sideways look. "You're a good egg, Sienna."

I nudge him playfully on the shoulder. "You say the strangest things. Are you sure you're not a time traveler from some corny past?"

Max's brows shoot up. "Maybe I am! My life would make so much more sense."

I laugh. This is the Max I know. "So, you forgive me?"

Max smiles. "Yes." He grows serious. "I guess I was mad that you didn't take my opinions seriously."

"Yeah, I should've noticed that you were more serious than you seem."

Max looks down with a small smile. "I guess I can be a lot sometimes." He looks at me sideways. "I'm not used to having a friend who I don't feel like I have to impress. My mom drags me around everywhere, and I always feel like I have to stand out to be noticed."

"It wasn't hard to notice you," I say. "You've been my first real friend since I moved here." *And I've learned something from you*, I think, but don't say out loud. I've learned I don't have to try to control every detail of my friendships, like I tried to do with my old friends. Everyone is actually their own person. Who knew?

He stands up. "Should we go back to the shed? Is that where that rehab lady is?"

"Yeah."

As we hop off the porch, I bump against him, and he bumps me back. It feels good to be friends again.

Car tires on gravel sound at the end of the driveway. A tightness grabs my chest, and I grip Max's arm. "My parents are here. I have to tell them about Persimmon."

Max's eyes widen. "Do you want me to stay with you?" Everything in his voice makes it clear he doesn't want to, but I don't want to face my parents alone. I'm comforted just knowing he's by my side.

"Please. And thank you."

Mom gets out of the car, glances at Max, and rushes over. "What are you doing out of school?"

"I'm okay," I say. "I can explain."

Mom and Dad exchange worried glances, then Mom's expression darkens. "What's going on now?"

Dad nods to Maite's Jeep. "Who's that?"

"There's a wildlife rehabilitator here; her name is Maite." My words pour out. "I wasn't honest with you when I said I didn't know anything about that fawn that Jules was playing with. Her name is Persimmon, and Jules found her a week ago, and I've been taking care of her in the shed since then."

My parents blink as they process what I said.

Dad is the first to recover. "You've been taking care of the fawn? In the shed? How?"

"She's still here. We found her in the woods last night after she ran away and brought her back."

Dad frowns. "Why would you do that? You know how I feel about deer."

"Persimmon isn't just any deer," I say. "She was

abandoned and about to be attacked by a coyote. She needed help. Let me show you." As we walk to the shed, I tell them all about the last week—how I figured out how to feed Persimmon and keep her safe, how Max helped, and how I finally went to Max's mother and the rehabilitator.

"Why didn't you come to us?" Mom asks, her voice a mixture of anger and hurt.

Dad puts his arm around my shoulder as we walk down the hill. "Sienna, what's really going on?"

At the touch, something crumbles in me and tears spill out. "I didn't want you to worry, because you have so much going on with the inn. I thought I could handle it myself. I'd already messed things up with the fire and the accreditors."

Dad stops and gives me a hug. "You never have to handle difficult things by yourself. That's what we're here for."

"But that's not true. You left me practically alone with the inn to run, along with Nainai."

"We left you in charge because you always handled everything so well; you are responsible and trust-worthy," Dad says.

I have so many pent-up feelings, it's hard to say what I want. "You never asked me how I felt."

Mom reaches out and hugs me. "You're right. We haven't been fair to you. We left you with a lot of responsibilities without checking to see how you were doing."

I lean into the hug, and Dad joins us in a group hug. Tears slip down my cheeks. Now that I'm in their arms I don't know why I didn't confide in them earlier. It feels so good to trust them with the whole story.

I wipe away my tears and look at my parents. "I did manage to take care of Persimmon." I glance over at Max, who's made himself as unobtrusive as possible. "Thanks to Max."

"But keeping a wild fawn isn't the same as taking care of a sheepadoodle," Dad says.

I nod. "I know that now."

Dad lets me go and nods toward the shed. "So, let's see this baby deer."

I lead my parents to the shed, where Persimmon is eating from the bottle Maite holds.

"Hello, you must be Sienna's parents." Maite straightens with a smile. "I'm Maite Santoja."

Mom gasps at Persimmon. "She's so tiny. How adorable . . . and look at that heart-shaped spot!" She glances at me. "You took care of her?" A look of admiration crosses her face, which makes me stand taller. I've been so scared of how my parents would react, and this is the last thing I'd imagined.

"She was even smaller when we first met her."

Jules pads over to us and licks Mom's hand. She rubs his head absently and a realization dawns on her. "The goats weren't really giving less milk. You were feeding this fawn with it." She shakes her head. "You made us worry needlessly."

"I'm sorry." I feel terrible. Now I see that every choice I'd made to hide Persimmon was mostly to save myself from being caught, instead of to help Persimmon or our family. "And I ruined everything with the accreditors."

"That wasn't on you," Dad says. "Sienna, we are the innkeepers, so we're responsible for our accreditation."

Dad has said this already, but this time it sinks in. I feel lighter.

"Mom and Dad, can we keep her? Maite said we

can if we build her an enclosure and she can give us advice on caring for her."

My parents look at Maite, who nods. "Normally, people who aren't certified aren't allowed to keep the fawns," she says, "but I can let you do it for a short while under my supervision."

"What would that involve?" Dad says.

As Maite explains how we'll need to provide a space outside that's protected and big enough, I slip out of the shed.

There is still one more thing I need to do.

CHAPTER TWENTY-TWO

"Where are you going?" Max has followed me out of the shed.

"Back to the inn. I have an email to write."

"What's the plan?"

I'm not sure I want to tell Max yet, not because I don't trust him, but because I don't want to jinx myself. "Would you hate me if I didn't tell you?"

Max smiles. "Nah. You're cool; I trust you." He jogs backward to his room, waving with his good arm. "Let me know if you want to go treasure hunting or hang out in the woods."

I grin back. "I will, in a bit." I head to the office and riffle through the loose papers and cards on the desk until I find what I'm looking for—the business card that the accreditors left with my parents.

I type up an email. After hovering my finger for a few long moments, I hit Send.

Now it's time to wait.

That evening, after the deer rehabber leaves,

my parents and I talk about whether I can keep Persimmon. I thought I'd have to argue with them and convince them, but they're surprisingly okay with the idea.

"We'll follow Maite's recommendations, and other than building the enclosure, you'll be completely responsible," Dad says.

"I promise to take the best care of her!" I hug them both tightly. I pull out my phone to check my emails and squeak when I see the reply from Jaime Martinez.

"What's that about?" Mom says.

"Don't be mad at me," I say. "This morning, I emailed the accreditor and asked if we could have another chance with another visit."

"You did that?" Mom gives me a hard stare. "I told you that this wasn't your issue. I don't think it was a good idea to contact him; that seems unprofessional."

"It's okay, because he said yes!" I say, before Mom can continue. "They're coming back in a few days."

Mom stares at me in astonishment. "What did you tell him to get them to reconsider?"

"I explained how the whole thing with Jules and Persimmon and the bad reviews was my fault, and that they shouldn't punish you for my mistake."

Mom's brow arches up. "You did it again, taking the weight of the world on your shoulders when you don't need to." She hugs me. "We're grateful, and yes, we'll be prepared this time."

"There's one more thing," I say. "I told them I'd like to speak to them when they get here. But I need to go to school late that day."

"Oh?" Mom gives me a skeptical look. "I don't know about that."

"Please, it's important. I want to help make the case for our inn, and I promise I won't let you down." I hold my breath and hope my parents will let me have this one last thing.

My parents look at each other, do that silent parental ESP thing, and Dad nods. "We'll talk to them too, of course, but you can say your piece as well. Let's get to cleaning; we've got a lot of work to do."

"Thank you, you're the best!" I go in for the second hug of the evening.

I work hard the next couple of days when I'm not at school to help my parents get the inn ready for the accreditors' visit. Dad builds an enclosure near the forest which includes trees and bushes, and he covers the fence with a dark green netting to shield Persimmon from the outside world. I ask Mom to take me to the craft store to get poster board.

On the morning the accreditors come, I bake chocolate chip cookies—this time without creating a small fire in the kitchen—and am ready. When Mr. Martinez and Ms. Hillsong show up, Mom and Dad welcome them to the living room, where Nainai and I are seated. The scrumptious smell of non-burnt cookies permeates the room.

"Hello, Sienna," Mr. Martinez says. "Thank you for your email."

"Thanks for hearing me out." I'm wearing my best outfit, and I've set up an easel with the poster board I've made. On it are pictures of Jules, Persimmon, the goats, and a photo of the forest behind our inn.

"I want to tell you a story about magic and friendship and connectedness," I begin.

Mom and Dad glance at me, looking slightly befuddled. My grandma pats my arm reassuringly. I haven't told anyone what I'm about to say, but I love how she's always there for me no matter what.

"A couple weeks ago," I begin, "my sheepadoodle, Jules, found a fawn that had lost her mother. She was weak and scared, and Jules made her feel safe. I took her in and fed her goat milk, and Jules and I tried our best to take care of her."

The accreditors look at each other and at me with puzzled expressions. Ms. Hillsong puts down her pen and says, "I'm sorry, I'm not following why this is relevant to our evaluation of the Rolling Hills Bed and Breakfast."

Mom and Dad shift uncomfortably. Mom looks like she's about to say something, but I give her a pleading look.

She shrugs, as if to say, *We trust you.*

"I have a reason for telling you this," I say. "While I was taking care of the fawn, we had two long-term guests," I continue. "Dr. Susan Klein and her son, Max, taught me about how trees are connected. The trees take care of each other through their roots, communicating through the use of fungi."

The man clears his throat. "This seems even more afield than the story of the fawn." He looks at his watch. "You'd better get to the point."

"I will." I go to the poster board and draw on it with a marker. I draw lines from the trees to the photos of Jules and Persimmon while I speak. "At first, I thought I could do everything by myself." I draw a stick figure of myself and scribble images of baking pastries, feeding Persimmon, and making towel animals. I become more animated as I go. "I tried to feed and take care of the fawn without telling my parents about her. I tried to keep up with the breakfast pastries and the farm chores and the housekeeping, and everything fell apart." I grimace at the memory. "You saw that when you came by the other day.

"But it turned out I wasn't really doing it by myself," I say. "Jules helped me with Persimmon more than anyone or anything else. He was by her side every day, calming her down and making her feel safe. He even brought food for her when she needed it. My friend Max took care of Persimmon when I was at school."

Mr. Martinez looks up, and Ms. Hillsong is rapt with attention, a half smile on her face.

"And then I learned that trees work together to defend each other and to feed each other, and to make every tree in the system grow stronger and better. That made me realize that that's what we're doing here at the inn too."

Dad smiles. He's getting it. Mom leans back, her posture more relaxed. I notice a movement at the doorway; Max has slipped in and listens with a wide smile.

I return his smile and continue. "My dad manages the farm animals and makes sure they're healthy. My mom uses our goat milk to make soaps and lotions to sell to our guests." I glance at Nainai. "My grandmother cooks and keeps the house clean. Jules protects our animals from raccoons, coyotes, and other animals that might try to eat them."

The man leans closer. "What about you, young lady? What's your role in the bed-and-breakfast?"

I smile and pull out the box I'd set aside earlier. "This is something my dog and I've gathered. Jules has found these things on our property." I hand the woman a coin and the man a shard of the pottery.

"What are these?"

"They're colonial artifacts on our property. I've cleaned them and researched them. We can display these, and also give our guests a chance to find their own artifacts." I smile. "We'll give them metal detectors, or let Jules be their guide.

"So you see," I say, "every one of us does our part to make this inn an amazing experience for our guests. That's where the magic happens. We build each other up and the sum is bigger than the parts."

Max pipes up from behind the couch and pumps his fists. "Yeah! That's right. The parts are bigger than the whole. The whole is bigger than the parts. Or something like that!"

The woman glances at him, startled. "And you are?"

I smile. "This is Max Klein. He and his mom are our long-term guests that I mentioned. He's my good friend."

Max lets his jaw drop open. "Good friend? What about great friend? The best of friends."

I laugh. "Yes, the best of friends." I gesture to my parents. "Anyway, my parents are the ones who do all the behind-the-scenes things that make the bed-and-breakfast run smoothly. I don't even know all of what they do, but the guests love it.

"I don't want you to punish my parents for my mess. Look at our reviews. But maybe not the last two reviews. Talk to our guests. Talk to my parents. It's not about me."

I sit down. I don't know if what I've said is enough. But it's the best I can do.

The man stands up. "Thank you, Sienna. It was very helpful to hear your presentation. It's unusual to overturn our previous decision, but in certain extenuating circumstances, it is possible."

I feel like jumping up and down, but I keep my excitement under the surface and just smile.

Mr. Martinez turns to my parents. "We'll be happy to meet with you now to go over some of your marketing and business plans."

Mom stands up. "Thank you. We're doing some innovative things and will be happy to tell you about them."

The adults head to the study to continue their discussion, leaving me with Nainai, Max, and Jules.

My grandma turns to me and pulls me into her arms. "You're the best, Sienna."

"You are, Nainai," I say, sinking into her hug.

"If you squeeze any tighter, I'm going to hurt my back again," Nainai says.

We both laugh.

On our way to check on Persimmon, Max says, "I heard you get to keep Persimmon. That's so awesome! She and Jules can play together all the time, and you'll have a new pet!"

I smile, but something feels off. When I'd told the inn accreditors about everyone pulling together to make the inn work, I'd missed something important. I'd made the case that my family and friends are like the fungi and trees that support one another, but who are Persimmon's supporters? The goats give her milk, Jules is her best friend, and Max and I take care of her physical needs.

But Persimmon really needs her own family of other fawns.

The lesson of the fungi and trees isn't just that different species help one another, but that the trees help their own family members.

My body thrums with the weight of that thought, and I sigh. "Persimmon is better off with the other fawns at Maite's place."

Max peers at me. "What are you saying? You don't think we can take care of her?"

"We can," I say, "but we'd be doing it for our own selfish reasons—because I want a friend for Jules or a pet deer."

"And what's wrong with that?"

"It's not what's best for Persimmon. I want her to grow up to be happy in the wild, and she'll be harder to release if she stays with us." Even as I say it, a pang shoots through me. I don't want to give up Persimmon, not after working so hard to care for her and keep her alive. Not after my parents even agreed to keep her.

Max nods thoughtfully. "You're right. So you made your dad build that enclosure for her and you're going to turn around and give her back?"

I bark out a laugh. "Yeah, they're going to think I'm a flake."

CHAPTER TWENTY-THREE

When I finally get up the courage to tell my parents that I've changed my mind, they're sitting on the porch, with Jules by their feet. I take a deep breath. "Mom, Dad, I know you agreed to let me take care of Persimmon." Even though I've made up my mind, it's still hard to say. "I think it's best to let Maite take her after all."

Mom's eyebrows raise. "Really? Are you sure?"

"You're testing our patience," Dad says, but with a smile in his voice.

I let out an unsteady breath. "It's just that I've thought about it and keeping Persimmon is what *I* want, but it's not what's best for her. I'm sorry you built the enclosure for nothing."

"It's not for nothing," Dad says, with a mysterious smile.

"What do you mean?"

"I spoke with Maite, and she agreed to let us volunteer with her over the summer and next year," Dad says. "If you're interested, she'll train us to become actual deer rehabilitators. I'll be an apprentice and train for it, because I'm the adult, but you can learn alongside me."

My jaw drops, and I leap up and into his arms. "Really? I'd love it!" I let go of him. "Wait, what happened to your hatred of deer? Who are you and what did you do with my dad?"

"The deer are here to stay, and I've got to get used to them. That little fawn of yours won me over with her cuteness." Dad smiles and winks at me. "Plus, I have you to do most of the work."

"Gladly!" I can't believe this turn of events, but a small hollow inside me remains. "But we should give Persimmon to Maite."

"You're right. She needs to learn to be a wild deer with the other fawns. When we're up and running as rehabilitators ourselves, we'll be able to house more than one fawn."

Even though it feels like my heart is scraped out from the inside, I know this is the right decision. One day, we'll be able to help other little fawns and see them grow strong enough to send out to the wild. But we don't have what Maite has now—experience, facilities, and other fawns.

Jules nudges me, and I bend down to give him a hug. Even my fluffy dog seems to know that he's about to lose his little deer friend. "I think we'll be okay," I whisper in his ear, and he turns and licks my cheek.

When Maite comes to pick Persimmon up, I blink back tears. "Can I give her one last hug?"

"We don't want to encourage human contact and bonding," Maite says, "but I'll make an exception this one time."

I go to Persimmon and run my hand along her little head and neck.

The little fawn nuzzles my neck, like she's kissing me. My heart melts for the umpteenth time. I wrap my arms around her and sprinkle kisses on her forehead.

"Stay well, Persimmon. Remember us." I look at Maite. "Can we come visit her?"

Maite nods. "Yes, but from afar. We want her to forget her human friends."

I bite my lip and nod.

Jules and Persimmon touch noses, then trade licks.

Persimmon picks up a stick and offers it to Jules. It's their favorite game! Jules knows exactly what to do. He bites one end of the stick while she holds on to the other end. They play tug-of-war, and Jules lets Persimmon win, as usual.

Persimmon drops the stick at Jules's feet and scampers around him.

He follows her. They run around in their game of tag. Jules touches his nose to encourage Persimmon. She runs away and then turns back playfully.

I could watch them forever, but I know it's time for them to say goodbye. I clap my hands. "Jules, come here."

Jules runs over with a big smile, Persimmon following behind.

Maite loads Persimmon into a crate and onto a truck.

Jules sticks his nose through the grate to say one last goodbye. He and Persimmon bump noses.

Max and his mom join us to see Persimmon off, watching Maite's truck bump down the driveway and turn onto the road and out of sight.

* * *

A couple of weeks later, it's time to say goodbye to Max and his mom. He and I go for one last walk in the woods.

"Look!" Max points.

Near an old stump, a circle of mushrooms has sprouted from the evening's rain.

Delight shoots through me. "It's a mushroom fairy ring! Have you seen them before? I've heard it's a sign of fairies dancing in a circle and will bring good luck."

Max grins. "Or it's a result of fungi living underground that form a circle due to their natural tendencies to find food."

"You're no fun, Max," I say. "Where's the magic?"

Max raises his brows in mock concern. "Sienna, you, a person who needs to know and control everything, a believer in magic and the unexplained?"

As we walk to the mushroom fairy ring, I knock into Max, shoulder to shoulder. "Maybe I'm more complicated than you think. You don't know everything about me."

I come to the circle and stand outside it. "Are you going to step in the ring?"

Max shakes his head. "No, even though it's a

completely natural phenomenon, I'm not going to risk the wrath of fairies."

We laugh.

I kneel close and run my fingers over the soft, velvety caps of the whitish-gray mushrooms. They seem both delicate and sturdy. As I take in the wonder of the mushroom ring, Jules bounds over and right through the ring.

"Whoa," Max says. "I guess Jules doesn't worry about fairies." He looks around and takes in a deep whiff of the forest air. "I'm going to miss this." He glances sideways at me and gives me a small smile. "You're pretty cool too. I've never met an artifact-collecting, fawn-caring innkeeper before."

Warmth rushes to my face. I'm going to miss him. "You're not so bad yourself. Hope you can visit us again."

Max's eyes glint as he breaks into a huge smile. "I probably will. My mom's planning to do the same research next year to follow up, whether or not the project is approved."

We walk in companionable silence, the crunch of leaves underfoot punctuated by the occasional chirps of birds.

When we return to the inn, Mom greets us with a grin. "Dad and I have a surprise for you. Let's go to the shed."

I look at Max, who shrugs. He's in the dark as much as I am.

Jules runs up to us and in and around our legs. He seems to sense that *Something very exciting is going on!* He runs ahead down to the shed, wagging his whole behind.

Mom opens the door and puts her finger to her lips. "Let's not be too loud."

As my eyes adjust to the dim interior, I see a large box with a bow on it inside the pen we'd used to take care of Persimmon.

"Go ahead, open it," Dad says with a smile.

My heart quickens. I don't know what's in the box, but Jules is going wild with excitement, circling it and wagging his tail so hard it might fall off, and my parents can barely contain themselves. Dad holds on to Jules's collar and nods.

I crouch by the box and lift the lid. I gasp.

Out pops the cutest little furry face—a sheepa-doodle puppy! It's a miniature and supercute version of Jules. Another living stuffed animal!

"Is this for us?"

"We got her for you," Mom says. "You took such good care of Persimmon, and once you decided to give her up, Dad and I talked and thought you could take care of this little one."

"It's a lot of work to train and take care of a puppy," Dad says.

"I'm up for it!" I'm thrilled. I hold out my hand to let the puppy get used to my scent. "And I have Jules to help me. He took such good care of Persimmon that I'm sure he'll be a perfect puppy parent."

"What are you going to name her?" Max asks.

I pick up the puppy and cuddle her. Her tiny tongue laps at my neck. I sit back on my heels. The puppy scrabbles and wants to climb all over me. "I don't know. I think we need to watch her for a while to see what her personality is like before naming her."

What I do know is I'm falling in love with this puppy already, and will love her as much as I do Persimmon. I bury my face in the wriggling puppy and give her the biggest hug.

CHAPTER TWENTY-FOUR

One year later

The inn's door chimes open and Jules runs to the door barking excitedly. Tulip, a slightly thinner and bouncier version of Jules, follows closely at his heels.

"Jules, my man! How've you been? It's been way too long. And you must be the puppy I met a year ago."

I lope up the stairs, grinning at the familiar sight, though his voice is not quite the same, cracking around the edges. "Max!" I stop short at the top of the steps. Since last summer, he's grown half a head taller than me.

He gives me a wide grin. "Sienna!"

After a brief moment of awkwardness, we go in for a hug, and it feels like no time has gone by since I've last seen him. I turn to his mom who's stepped in. "Hello, Dr. Klein. So glad you're here with us again!"

"Me too." Dr. Klein smiles. "I see you got your star! Good thing I booked us far in advance."

"Yeah." I beam. "We found out at the end of summer last year."

"Thanks to you and your presentation, I'm sure," she says.

I was so proud when we'd gotten the star. After that, bookings at our inn went way up, Mom and Dad raised our prices, and we got the loan. We have reliable Wi-Fi now, and we renovated the barn, where we host art and collectible fairs.

"Max, I want to show you something." I grab him by the arm and pull him to the back.

Jules perks up and follows us. Tulip runs around in circles.

"Don't mind me. I'll get myself settled," Dr. Klein says, smiling.

As Max and I walk down the hill past the goat barn and the shed where we took care of Persimmon last summer, he looks at me quizzically. "What's going on?"

I smile. "We have to be quiet." I pick up a stick as we walk over to a log in the grassy area near the trees and sit down.

Max joins me. Jules and Tulip sit by us; they both know to be quiet.

"She comes around this time almost every day."

"Who comes?" Max says a little too loudly.

"Shhh. You'll see."

After about ten minutes, with Max only fidgeting a bit, a rustle comes from the woods.

"It's a deer!" Max says softly, under his breath. He turns to me. "Is it who I think it is?"

I nod and break into a grin. "Yes. It's Persimmon!"

A beautiful and stately looking deer comes out of the trees. Even though she lost her little white heart spot by the end of last summer, she and her family members often visited the wildlife rehabber's place during the winter, so I know her well. A few weeks ago, I was overjoyed when she showed up at our woods.

Now Jules runs up to her, and the two greet each other joyfully. Both of their tails wag wildly, and they lick each other. I hold on to Tulip, who wants to join them, but I want to make sure Jules and Persimmon enjoy their reunion.

Jules and Persimmon chase each other in the grass, just like they used to last summer. Jules runs up to me and I hand him the stick, which he takes to Persimmon. They start tussling with it, like they used to.

I let Tulip go, and she joins in the fun. The three of them scamper about, until Persimmon stops and touches her nose to each of my dogs. Jules and Tulip stand at attention with their tails wagging.

Persimmon makes a low honking sound. After a moment, she repeats it.

My eyes widen. Behind Persimmon, two adorable ears peek out from the grass. I stand up to get a better look. "Persimmon brought a fawn to meet us!"

The fawn bleats a *weah*.

Persimmon stands proudly by a small fawn and shows off her baby to Jules.

Max, Tulip, and I watch from the log. I don't want to spook Persimmon, who hovers protectively by her baby.

Jules approaches the fawn gently and touches his nose to the fawn's. The fawn looks up and then at its mom, as if for reassurance, and Persimmon bends her head close to both Jules and the fawn.

The fawn toddles closer to Jules, and Jules gives it a gentle lick.

I grip Max's arm. His face is filled with the same

awe and delight that I'm sure is on my own. Tiny and vulnerable Persimmon has turned into a proud and strong momma deer. And like Persimmon when she was a fawn, this baby has a heart-shaped white spot on her side!

Jules comes back and leads Tulip to Persimmon and her fawn, and it's as if he's showing off his own family. The younger sheepadoodle sniffs the fawn, and soon, all four are playing and dancing together.

Surrounded by my dearest friends—Jules, Tulip, Max, Persimmon and her fawn—my heart is about to burst from joy.

Author's Note

Although Sienna took in an abandoned baby fawn in this story, most baby fawns that are found in the wild or in backyards are not abandoned by their mothers and should be left alone. A mother deer will look for food while leaving her fawn for long periods of time. The fawns are hidden in long grass, their spots helping keep them safe. As Sienna learns, if a fawn is injured or really abandoned, the best thing to do is to call a licensed wildlife rehabilitator, who will know how to take care of the animal.

In the story, Sienna learns about how trees cooperate and communicate with one another through chemicals shared through the mycorrhizal fungi network. Some books that discuss this topic include *Finding the Mother Tree: Discovering the Wisdom of the Forest* by Suzanne Simard (Vintage Books, 2021) and *The Hidden Life of Trees: What They Feel, How They Communicate: Discoveries from a Secret World* by Peter Wohlleben (translated by Jane Billinghurst, William Collins, 2017). Some scientists believe the theories that trees cooperate with one another are simplistic and that ecosystems are complicated, since trees also compete with one another for light and food.

Any errors in this story are my own.

Acknowledgments

Like the trees in a forest, I'm surrounded by a wonderful community that's made this story possible.

Thank you to my editor, Maya Marlette, who once again made the process so fun. I'm in awe of your insights and deft editorial eye. Many thanks to the Scholastic team, including Maeve Norton and Diego Salas for the cover; the production editor, Melissa Schirmer; the copy editor and proofreaders, Hannah Calderazzo, Olivia Valcarce, Lisa Liu, and William Franke; Rachel Feld, Katie Dutton, Greyson Corley, Victoria Velez, Erin Berger, Seale Ballenger, Sabrina Montenigro, Emily Heddleson, and Lizette Serrano for Marketing and Publicity; and the entire Sales team including Elizabeth Whiting, Jarad Waxman, Dan Moser, Nikki Mutch, Tracy Bozentka, and Savannah D'Amico.

I'm grateful for my agent, Jennifer March Soloway, for always supporting me and providing great advice.

One of my favorite parts of writing this book was learning fascinating information from experts. I learned about deer and fawn rehabilitation from wildlife rehabilitators Cindy Lakan and Brian Rooney; tree ecology and sustainable forestry farming from Kathryn Gaglione and Neil Hughes; Virginia forests from Ashley Appling, Extension Agent—Horticulture, Virginia Cooperative Extension, Culpeper County Office; field research methods from Cole Grannan, graduate student at the University of Northern Colorado; sheepadoodle insights from Kimberley Losey and Victoria Piontek; and running a bed-and-breakfast from Nance and Tom Mazzola of Hill of Content Bed & Breakfast and Louise Wood at The Bed & Breakfast at Peace Hill Farm.

My writing community always sustains me. Thank you, Teresa Robeson, Hannah Capin, Jessica Grace Kelley, Brittany Page, and Rachel Parris, for helping make this story shine. Thank you, Alysa Wishingrad, for being my sounding board and always reminding me of "agency" and "stakes." Much love to the Sprintlings (yay, Kate, Yvette, Alyssa, Caroline, Erica, Melissa, and Alysa), MG Authorcade, and many more who've enriched my writing journey.

As always, I couldn't have done this without the constant love and support of my family, David, Sammi, Sarah, my parents, and my in-laws, Susan and Alan.

Thank you, "deer" readers: May you all find your community to uphold and support you.

About the Author

Sylvia Liu grew up with books and daydreams in Caracas, Venezuela. Once an environmental attorney, she now spins stories inspired by nature, adorable animals, and strong girls. Her middle grade books include *Manatee's Best Friend* and *Hana Hsu and the Ghost Crab Nation*, and her picture book, *A Morning with Grandpa*, illustrated by Christina Forshay, was a New Voices Award winner. Sylvia lives in Virginia with her family and a fluffy cat.